Being Dad

SHORT STORIES ABOUT FATHERHOOD

Tangent Books

Being Dad: Short Stories About Fatherhood
First published 2016 by Tangent Books

Tangent Books
5.16 Paintworks, Bristol BS4 3EH
0117 972 0645
www.tangentbooks.co.uk
Email: richard@tangentbooks.co.uk

ISBN 978-1-910089-32-3

Authors: Dan Powell, Toby Litt, Courttia Newland, R.J. Price, Tim Sykes, Rodge Glass, Iain Robinson, Nicholas Royle, Nikesh Shukla, Richard W. Strachan, Richard V. Hirst, Dan Rhodes, Lander Hawes, Andrew McDonnell, Samuel Wright

Editor: Dan Coxon

Cover Design: Mike Best

Design: Joe Burt (www.wildsparkdesign.com)

A CIP record of this book is available at the British Library.

Printed on paper from a sustainable source

Contents

Introduction

WHEN WE FIRST CONCEIVED OF THIS ANTHOLOGY OF fatherhood-themed fiction, we weren't sure which market to pitch it at. Would only fathers be interested? Might mothers find it illuminating too? Would there be any interest from the childless? From single readers?

We needn't have worried. As soon as we announced our intentions, it became clear that the readership for *Being Dad* was far more wide-ranging than we'd imagined. Some readers who've contacted us have expressed an interest specifically in the book's theme – treating it almost as a fictional fatherhood manual – but many others have been drawn by the promise of new short stories by some of the most exciting fiction writers around. The fact that all fifteen of these writers are also fathers only makes these tales all the more immediate and relevant.

Of course, it helps that we have such talented writers attached to the project. Within these pages you'll find new stories by Toby Litt, Nikesh Shukla, Dan Rhodes, Courttia Newland and Nicholas Royle, all of whom are well known and respected in the short fiction field. Toby's story is a particular treat, revisiting the characters from his critically-acclaimed collection *Life-Like*. Dan Powell has already made a name for himself too, with his debut collection *Looking Out of Broken Windows* being shortlisted for numerous awards, while Rodge Glass has rapidly become one of the most exciting practitioners of the short art. Finally, R.J. Price has a short story collection and a novel to his name, but is also an acclaimed poet. These authors alone should be enough to make you start turning these pages.

Then there are the emerging writers that we're showcasing here, some of them already achieving acclaim in the field. When we accepted Richard W. Strachan's story we had no idea that he would be shortlisted for the Manchester Writing Prize later in the year. Lander Hawes, Andrew McDonnell, Iain Robinson and Tim Sykes are all part of the vibrant and thriving short story scene in and around Norwich at the moment, a scene that seems certain to produce several new literary stars. Richard V. Hirst and Samuel Wright are already creating names for themselves too. Anyone who keeps an eye on the small presses will have enjoyed their work in recent years. We can't claim to have unearthed these authors, but hopefully we're helping to bring them to a new – and admiring – audience. Their words will be more than enough to win you over.

This book couldn't have happened without the support of everyone who backed our crowdfunding campaign. We needed a show of interest, as well as a demonstration of faith, and you gave us both. Particular thanks go to Dr. Roger Banks and Shaun Buhre, whose generosity literally brought this book into being. I hope you're as proud of it as we are.

Dan Coxon
Editor

A Father's Arms

Dan Powell

JABS. BABY ANNA'S FIRST. NOT MINE. ALREADY BEEN through this twice before with the boys. Old hand by now. A slab-faced nurse hurries us into a cluttered exam room. First thing she says: Mummy not with you? She's looking at Anna but speaking to me. I say nothing for a moment. Concentrate on unclipping Anna from her car seat.

Mum doesn't like needles, I say once Anna is huddled on my lap.

I unwrap her from her babygro, flick the poppers open with the fingers of my free hand, careful not to pull or pinch her chubby legs. Anna gurgles, a thick, wet, joy-filled sound. The nurse waves vaccine bottles at me, explains she'll be giving two injections, one in each thigh.

Diphtheria, Whooping Cough, Tetanus, Polio, and Hib in one, she says, Pneumococcal in the other.

I nod, shuffle Anna over my lap until she is lying across me, rest her head in the crook of my elbow. I wrap my left hand around her left thigh. Lock my fingers without squeezing. I'm about to roll her gently to one-side, raise and grip her right thigh ready for the needle, when the nurse, her tone rough and sharp as a brick, says, You need to hold her properly.

She steps forward, needle in one hand, other outstretched,

about to take Anna's leg.

You must keep her still.

The nurse's words are shrill and brittle. Her eyes brim with exasperation that spills over me. Her thought is in her face: another hapless dad forced to bring baby by an over-sensitive mum. I meet her exasperation with my own.

I was about to, I say and roll Anna smoothly up onto her side, take her right leg in my right hand. I keep my voice cool. Make my words blunt objects. I've done this before, I say. Many times. She's got two brothers.

The nurse huffs. Her body judders, disgruntled. For a moment she looks unsure of what to do next, then steps closer. Sickly perfume wafts from her. Anna's nose wrinkles, her little brow furrows. I smile, let loose a small snorting laugh, mostly through my nostrils. Fix my eyes on Anna as the first needle goes in, watch the shock of it blast through her fierce blue eyes. Her wail, when it comes, is thin and reedy, like a cat's and it drowns out all other sound. So different from the stocky shouts of her brothers back when it was their turn. I stroke her cheek. Whisper softly in her ear. Roll her onto her other side. Grip her left leg ready for round two. The nurse is quick and slips the second needle in before Anna's wailing has chance to stop.

She'll likely get a bit of a temperature, nothing Calpol won't sort, maybe sleep a little more.

I nod at the nurse as I wrap Anna back up, strap her back in her seat. As we are shown out, Anna, already settled, blows a raspberry at nothing in particular.

That night a nudge to my ribs wakes me. Green alarm clock

digits tell me it is after two. Anna's thin feline wail streams
down the landing.

Your turn, Aimee says and rolls over.

I am sure it was my turn last night too, but Aimee has
work tomorrow and I don't. With luck Anna will make up
some sleep in the day and then I will too. Quiet steps down the
landing. Past the boys' room. Simon, our eldest, is at the door
of the room he shares with his brother. He is all sticky-up hair
and rubs his eyes with the balls of his palms

Whass happin, he mumbles in half-sleep.

Just your sister, go back to bed.

Too noisy.

Won't be in a minute. Go back to bed.

Before I finish my words Anna stops. The pair of us, Simon
and I, hold our breath, listen for the baby to catch her own and
the wailing to begin again. It does not. I usher Simon back
into his room. He shambles toward his bed, his head nodding
a little with each step.

That's a good lad. I'll come back and tuck you in.

I do not find Anna asleep. She is alert and in the arms of
my father who is sat in the frayed armchair Aimee and I use
for night feeds.

She was starting to think you weren't coming, he says.
Anna has the knuckle of his forefinger in her mouth and is
gumming it. Saliva trails run over his worn, callused skin. He
looks up at me.

Is she teething?

Her immunisations probably. Or just time for her feed? I'll
put a bottle on.

I slip down stairs and flick the kettle on, snatch a bottle
from the fridge, half-sink it in an oversize beaker of boiled

t to feed her? I ask once back upstairs.

er's eyes light up and he nods. I wouldn't take any notice, he says once Anna is guzzling.

Any notice?

Of that nurse today.

His knowing about this stuff catches me off guard again.

I didn't, I say, but he shakes his head.

Yes you did. Shouldn't let it get to you. Back when you and your sister were little, folks really weren't that used to seeing a bloke deal with babies. I used to have to put up with all sorts of rubbish.

You already told me, I say. When you were really here you said all this. You were a new man before all that new man crap in the Eighties. I know.

There's sharpness in my voice, and I can feel bluntness in my expression. He looks up at me, waits to be sure I've finished.

Your point being, he says.

Tell me something I didn't already know before the boys were born, something you might tell me if you were here, I mean really here, to ask.

Anna finishes with the bottle and he lifts her to his shoulder pats her back. I wait for him to reply but he is busy whispering in my daughter's ear, his voice too quiet to hear. Anna's burp fills the room for a moment then he holds her out to me. A spatter of milk-white sick slowly soaks into the shoulder of his robe.

She might need a change, he says.

I take Anna and lay her on her change mat. When I look back to the chair, he is gone.

*

Dinner time. Aimee and I washing-up together, the kids still at the table finishing their meals. The boys push scraps of fish finger and barely touched puddles of peas about their plates. Baby Anna has dumped her food onto the tray of her high chair, made tiny mountains of mashed vegetables and meat. She pushes her fists into it, scoops it, watches it squeeze between her fingers. All the time laughing. I don't try and stop her, focus instead on clearing the cooking pots. We'll clean her up in a minute.

Aimee nudges me and smiles. Quality time, she says and winks.

I look down at my yellow washing up gloves. Not that sexy, I say.

Oh, I don't know.

I look up at this and catch the tail end of her grin and then Adam, our middle child, our youngest boy, only four, is crying. His hand covers his face. He wails.

What's the matter? What's happened? We speak in adult chorus, cross the kitchen together, stand either side of him, and crouch. What's the matter Adam?

He's put a pea up his nose, his older brother says. He is grinning.

Okay, okay. I turn Adam on his chair, away from the table, get him to face me.

He'll need to go to the hospital. You'll have to drive him. I had the last of the wine, Aimee says, her voice racing.

He doesn't need to go to the hospital. It'll come out.

I twist my head and try to peer up his nose but see nothing.

I smile at Adam, say softly, Adam, did you put something up your nose?

Pea. He blurts the word between held sobs. Pea. Pea. Hurts.

You need to get him to A&E. He could breathe it down into his lungs.

Aimee is pacing. Always surprises me, in every other instance, she remains calm, doesn't matter how drastic, but the slightest thing with the kids and it's red alert, action stations, worst case scenario.

Hold on. Let me have a proper look.

We clear the plates, empty the table and I lay him down on it, arch his head back. I swipe and tap the torch function of my phone, shine it up both nostrils. There's a glimmer of something dark and green in the left one. Either a pea or a giant bogey.

I think I see it. Have you got some tweezers? Longer the better.

Aimee fetches some from upstairs. They are short and their sharp-ends are not much smaller than his nostril.

I'll go and ask Lynne. She might have something better.

Lynne is the nurse who lives two doors down. She checks her first aid box and comes back to the door with a nine-inch surgical pair, still sterile-wrapped.

Do you need a hand getting it out? she says.

She comes back with me. Adam is still on the table but sat up. He sobs in quiet, tight little whimpers. I whisper in his ear and he lies back down.

Lynne holds his head still. Aimee holds my phone-torch. I rip the tweezers from the plastic and check the ends: thin and blunt. I jab the flesh of my forefinger in between the base of the prongs to open them wide enough to grab the pea.

Don't poke it up? Aimee blurts as I am about to insert the tweezers.

I don't look at her, look instead as far up my youngest son's nostril as I can. No, I say, I won't.

I slip the tweezers in, twist my head to see. No one speaks. Kitchen becomes operating theatre. Even Anna picks up on the emotional atmosphere and is quiet. I don't feel the pea so much as sense it, and slip my finger from between the prongs. The fact they do not close tells me they have something. I slide them out. Pinched between the tips is a single, bright green garden pea. A couple of looks up each nostril to be sure and the room breathes a sigh of relief.

Is that better? Adam nods and smiles and I show him the pea. See, Daddy got it?

Can I keep it?

You only put the one up there didn't you?

He nods.

Mummy'll put it in a tub for you. But you mustn't ever do that again.

He nods again.

That night, as he sleeps, the pea sits in the corner of a transparent plastic tub on his bedside table.

Later. Closing up the house. Doors locked. Lights off. Cooker off. Heating set for the right time in the morning. Check the kids. Simon, lamp still on, fast asleep, stretched out on the top bunk of his room. Books blanket the bed around him, an encyclopaedia of superheroes, *How To Draw Fantasy Creatures*, a Space Marines novel spread-eagled where its fallen from his hands as he slipped into sleep. Adam, slim frame tucked up tight under his duvet, his arms wrapped around his Doggy, boy and cuddly nose to nose. He is thinner than the other two and always feels the cold. In her room, Anna shuffles in her sleep-bag, the whisper of a dream frowning through her features, just visible in the pale wash of her nightlight.

Someone has left the hoover in the hall and I snatch it up as I pass so that no one will trip over it in the morning rush to school and work. I find my father sat in the under stairs cupboard. He is drawing heavily on a half-smoked cigarette. I breathe in, expecting the bitter smoke to awaken my own long-quit addiction but, despite the smoke that hangs in a thick fug in the slanted space beneath the stairs, I smell nothing.

How is the little lad?

He's fine. Something and nothing.

You used to do stuff like that all the time. Stuff up your nose, stuff in your ears.

I know.

One time, when you were potty training, your mum found you playing with your own shit. All up your arms, all over your clothes, your face. Cheeks covered in it.

He takes a last drag, stubs his cigarette out in a brown glass ashtray that I only now notice he is holding.

We never did know if you'd eaten any of it. Your mum thought you might have but you were too young to be able to tell us. I suppose you don't remember any of that.

I shake my head. I only remember them telling the story of it. How I sneaked my potty into the kitchen while Mum was hoovering in the hall. How she came in to find me under the table, shit everywhere. We've cleaned up plenty of sick and piss and shit streaked sleep-suits in our time as parents, Aimee and I, but at least none of ours have done anything like that. Though, with Anna, there's still time.

They keep you on your toes, he says.

Yes.

Aimee's voice calls: What are you doing down there?

I look up. She is leaning over the bannister, watching me.

Nothing, I say.

When I look back to the cupboard, my father, the smoke and the ashtray have all dispersed.

*

The night Anna is born, Aimee and I both remark on how perfectly round her head is compared to the squeezed asymmetry of her brothers' skulls post-delivery. The first weeks pass. The five bones that make up Anna's new-born skull, two frontal, two parietal, one occipital, start to shift. We learn these names and more in the weeks and months that follow. The dome of her head soon slopes to a lopsided point. She will only feed from one side and cannot turn her head from left to right without help.

The midwife refers us to our GP. Our GP refers us to a paediatrician. The paediatrician prescribes biweekly physiotherapy. Anna on a mat, her legs extended and manipulated, her arms raised and pulled gently across her chest, her body rolled. Homework exercises, three times a day to help build upper body strength. At the end of the first six-week slot of physio the paediatrician suggests helmet therapy.

More appointments. London this time. Long drives, followed by long waits as Anna is examined and measured. She is fitted with a nylon cap that presses her hair tight to her head, accentuating the shape of her skull. I lift her into a foam seat that grips her thighs and bottom and holds her in place. I hold her arms and keep her from moving. She must be still for the 3D camera to capture an accurate model of her head. Soon a virtual model of Anna's head rotates on the monitor, her asymmetry starkly rendered in what looks like pale-yellow dough. Looking down from above her skull is curved like a peanut.

We are shown an example of the helmet they will craft from Anna's data. A polished white exterior with a thick rigid foam lining that will be moulded to the shape of her head as it should be, ready for Anna to grow into. It will restrict the growth of her skull in places, allow it in others. It takes two weeks to make. At the fitting, the specialist trims the solid foam lining in places, peels thin slices from it, cuts it to size. Once on, it looks like the head gear of a sparring boxer. Anna's bright blond hair sprouts through the oval crown hole of the helmet top.

We take Anna, wearing the helmet, to the playroom and the cafeteria. We have ninety minutes to kill before her final fitting check. Within five she is clawing at it, pushing the nape of it up off her neck, jamming her fingers under the curves that scoop over each ear. She howls when it will not budge. She refuses to settle, refuses to eat.

After lunch, the final fitting. The specialist removes the helmet. Anna's hair is plastered to her skull, all except the tonsure of blond fluff that has been cupped in the hole at the top of the helmet. Already her baby smell is gone, replaced with the thick chemical tang from the cleaning alcohol used to sterilise the lining. She will be allowed to remove the helmet for thirty minutes each day. It will be cleaned while she is bathed and her hair washed. She will wear the helmet at all other times, morning and night, awake and asleep.

She'll get used to it in a day or two, the helmet specialist says.

I won't, says Aimee in the car on the drive home.

I search the internet and find a woman in America who designs and sells tough vinyl stickers for decorating these helmets. Two weeks later the letters A,n,n,a and the words Every Princess Wears A Crown, along with a shower of pink and purple flowers and a large pink crown, arrive on glossy card.

I sit at the kitchen table and set to. The boys are in their room, playing Lego. Aimee is bathing Anna. Squeals and splashes trickle down the stairs. My father is sat with me. I concentrate on arranging the stickers, but he insists on talking.

The posterior fontanelle usually closes between one and three months after birth, he says. The sphenoidal fontanelle is next to close, after about six months.

I don't answer, just concentrate on peeling the crown design from the glossy backed card, careful not to rip the elaborate crenellations of pink vinyl. I smooth it down, paste a thin layer of Mod Podge to fix it in place.

The mastoid and the anterior fontanelles close somewhere between six to nineteen months after birth, he says. The anterior is generally the last to close, mind.

I arrange her name, Anna, over the crown. Already the back of the helmet carries the words Every Princess Wears a Crown, and is spotted with pink and purple blooms, their thick petals framing the slogan.

The ossification of the bones of the skull is usually

complete after about eighteen months, my father says.

Which is why the paediatrician was so keen to have Anna seen so quickly. Helmet therapy works best the earlier it begins. The helmet immediately changes people's reactions to Anna though. We see them look with sympathy, sometimes fear. One of the boys' teachers asks if she is in pain and I explain. I stick to the key words and phrases. Helmet therapy. Asymmetry. A template in which her skull will shape itself. I wonder what they imagine, that her head would slip apart without the helmet to hold the pieces in place?

My father says, Lots of parents worry needlessly that their baby might be prone to injury at the fontanelles. They might be called soft spots, but they are extremely tough.

I paste Mod Podge over the last of the stickers and fasten up the jar. I am about to tell him to stop wittering through everything I've already read myself on Wikipedia and tell me something useful, when Aimee comes in, Anna wrapped in a towel.

Look what Daddy's made for you, she says and sits in the chair my father has already vacated.

I unvelcro the clasp of the helmet, place it over Anna's blow dried hair, and that quick the smell of the cleaning alcohol soaked into the rigid lining overpowers the smell of baby shampoo. I wiggle the helmet in place and refasten the clasp.

There, I say, don't you look beautiful.

*

Early summer. Driving to collect the boys from Cubs. Sun washes across the windscreen, slips past the lowered visor, dazzles. Baloo is at the door of my car before I can get out. His face a mask of concern.

There's been an incident, he says.

I'm out of the car. Only half-listening. Scanning the playing field outside the scout hut for my boys. Adam is running and shouting with the pack. I don't see Simon.

Another boy was throwing sticks and Simon was hit. Cut his eyebrow. Looked like it needed stitches so Bagheera took him straight to A&E. We tried to call you but we couldn't get through on either number.

Our home line, BT, has been out of action for much of the week, awaiting an engineer. I check my mobile. No Service.

He's all right though? Simon? He's okay?

He's fine, they only left about five minutes ago. You'll probably catch them.

I grab Adam and we drive across town to A&E. I park the car. At the pay and display machine I realise I have no change, just notes and bank cards. There's a number for payment by mobile but my phone still says No Service.

Fuck, I say, and Adam gasps and then giggles.

Daddy said a naughty word, don't copy Daddy, I say.

I leave the car without paying or displaying and drag Adam up the hill.

Simon is already in a treatment room. A nurse shows us in. A crooked gash arcs above his right eyebrow. The wound is clean but there is blood soaked into the collar of his Cub polo shirt and jumper, stains on his badges. Bagheera, a local gym instructor called Mark, is holding Simon's hand as a male nurse sutures the wound.

There you go, says Bagheera, your Dad's here. Told you he wouldn't be long.

Simon's eyes flick at me, then back to the nurse.

I should let your Dad sit down, says Bagheera, and he makes to move, makes to pull his hand from Adam's. But Adam keeps his grip, does not let go, does not look at me.

Bagheera retakes his seat. He shrugs at me. A confused look moves over his features.

It's okay, I say, let him be.

The nurse looks to Bagheera, then to me. Best he stays still anyway, he says.

Afterwards, I sign the paperwork. I see a shared look move between the nurse and the cub leader as Simon sits on a chair beside me but does not speak. I think I see suspicion. The nurse is making notes on Simon's paperwork. I want to ask what he is writing but can't.

There'll likely be a little scar. You might want to get some hydrating gel to rub in daily. And you'll need to make an appointment with your Practice Nurse for the end of the week. To have the stitches removed.

The nurse hands me his discharge paperwork. I see him see Simon refuse my hand as we leave the treatment room. Bagheera follows us out.

Thanks for bringing him down. Sorry you couldn't get hold of me, or my wife. I wave my phone at him. Never any service when you really need it.

He nods. He smiles. You okay now Simon? He is looking right at my son. Like he's watching for something.

Simon nods.

He's probably hungry. And tired, I say. Best get the pair of them home. Thanks again.

I usher the boys out through the sliding doors. Back to the car. Check my watch. Nearly an hour since we parked.

I expect to find a ticket waiting for me, but there isn't one. I wonder if the car park is camera controlled.

On the drive home Simon is quiet.

Have I upset you? I ask.

He mutters something I can't make out.

What was that? Can't hear you over the car and the traffic.

I take my eyes from the road for a second, take in the scowl that flares across features once so like my own, more like his mother's now.

What took you so long? he says.

The kids in bed, Aimee at her desk marking, I take a beer into the garden. Sit and watch the last of the sun slip behind the rooftops of the village. Anxiety bundles between my shoulder blades. I stretch. Expand my chest. Squeeze my shoulders together. Try to pop the bubble of tension building there.

I wouldn't take it to heart. They weren't thinking what you think they were thinking.

My father is beside me on the bench, his thick, work-hardened fingers wrapped round a pint of bitter. He takes a swig. The creamy head leaves a frothy moustache on his top lip. He wipes it with the back of his hand.

I know, I say.

You probably don't remember but back when you were three or four, you and your brother tipped that old wooden bench we had in the garden, right smack onto the big toe of your left foot. The doctors thought I'd done it. Thought I'd stamped on your foot. Tried to take me down the corridor, talk to me away from you, you away from me.

My father tells me this but I already know the story. I

don't really remember; just remember being told the story growing up.

You wouldn't have it though. You ran down that hospital corridor, right at me, threw yourself up into my arms, your arms around my neck and kissed my cheek. Can we go home now Daddy? you said, your black and blue toe dangling against my belly. I looked that doctor in the face. Does it look like I go about stamping on his feet? I said.

The image hangs there between us for a moment: my three year old, four year old self huddled up in his strong arms as he marches me out of the hospital.

Anyone who knows you, knows your kids, anyone with any bloody sense, knows you'd never hurt them.

But my thoughts jump track to those stories in the news all the time, of parents wrongfully accused, of children taken from homes when they should not have been. I can't help but think about how, if it can happen to someone, it can happen to anyone.

I look to my father for something more, for something else, something I never heard him say in life. But the seat beside me is empty.

*

Another year, another hospital. This time Adam. Only just turned two. Mid-January. Cold winter. What looks like a bad cold turns out, the GP says, his face serious, his tone urgent, to be pneumonia. I drive him straight to the hospital. Call Aimee at work and ask her to collect pyjamas and toothbrush, slippers and Doggy and meet me there. She arrives to find Adam wearing an oxygen mask, his little chest rising and falling, rising and falling, rising and falling, fast, fast, fast. First come the tears, then the questions.

Why didn't you take him to the doctor's sooner?

How could you miss something so serious?

Why didn't you check his temperature more carefully?

Each *you* hits hard. Shakes me. I knee-jerk at them, tell her it's not fair to just blame me.

I said we, she says, I said how could we miss it?

I hear the we now, but my own voice, echoing inside me, still says you. You. You. You missed this.

He is on the ward for a week and we take it in turns. I stay with him, then she stays with him, then I stay with him. Parental relay. Passing ships. We handover late evening, Simon trails home with whoever's turn it is to try get some rest. Anna has not yet joined us. Our four has yet to become a five.

My second night in hospital with him, Adam is in my arms. He breathes slower now but still too fast. The antibiotics are beginning to work. The foldaway bed I am lying on is too short and my feet stick out over the end like a child's. It is late and the corridors and wards outside are quiet. He nuzzles into me. In the lights from the car park outside, I watch a dream play out behind his brow. I stroke his cheek and his mouth wrinkles with a half-smile. He moves through layers of sleep, finds a deeper rest and settles. The rise and fall, rise and fall, rise and fall of his chest is now his only movement. I probe his palm with my index finger, and he grips it. We fit. I hold my baby boy and he holds me.

I listen to him breathe and think of the night Simon was born. Another hospital panic. A twenty-seven hour labour ending in an epidural; preparation for a C-section in case Simon could not be delivered with forceps and Venteuse.

Meconium indicating baby was in distress. Time quickened. Everything happened in snapshot.

Outside, phoning family quickly before Aimee is taken to theatre.

Hurrying back along the ancient, almost subterranean central corridor back to Salisbury Hospital's maternity wards, desperately wishing everything be okay.

In the changing room, getting dressed for theatre.

Feeling ridiculous in the gown and gloves and mask.

Back with Aimee, holding her hand again.

Walking next to her as the bed is wheeled to the operating room.

Urging Aimee to push in unsynchronised chorus with the nurses.

One nurse, her hand on Aimee's belly, feeling for contractions, the ultimately unnecessary epidural having robbed Aimee of sensation.

The crowning.

Then a full head, bawling and gore-streaked.

A baby thrust out.

Cleaned and checked and placed in my arms.

Staring into the eyes of my first child, my first son.

Simon blinking and squinting at the bright world that confronts him.

Me saying: His eyes, he's got amazing eyes.

Babbling, desperate to share these first moments with Aimee, to make up for stealing the first cuddle with our son.

Baby Simon still bawling, protesting the brightness of the maternity room, the openness of it.

Me holding him close as he mourns the loss of the womb.

Now, here in another hospital, the memories of Simon feel

as present as Adam in my arms. These memories are burnt into the brain, emotion as bright behind closed eyes as after images of the sun. Parenthood is all present tense.

The next night, my turn at home, Simon already bathed and in bed. I sit at the kitchen table, single place laid in front of me. A ready-meal warms in the oven, will be another ten minutes. I stay in the kitchen chair rather than slouch to the sofa and TV. The hard wooden chair and the cool kitchen floor against my bare feet help fight my bone tiredness. Between Adam's restlessness, nurses checking his temperature and fluids every few hours, and the night noises of the other patients on the ward, there is little sleep to be had in the hospital.

I rest my head in my hands, bare elbows on the wood of the table. I am far from comfortable but still my eyes creep shut.

I feel my father step behind me. He does not speak at first, just puts a hand on my shoulder. A squeeze. Then:

It'll be okay.

I hear the words, like I heard them back when he was alive. But even he doesn't sound convinced right now. I slump a little more. My head sags. His fingers squeeze the muscle of my neck again. Gently.

I'm about to tell him that he could have died, Adam could have died. He's only two and little kids have died of pneumonia, little kids still do die of pneumonia, thousands of them, millions, all over the world, for hundreds and thousands of years. He could have died and it would have been my fault. The words are burning in my throat, bubbling up, about to boil over, when the timer on my phone beeps to tell me my dinner should be ready.

I haul myself up from the kitchen chair. There is no one behind me.

*

The snip. A month and a year after Anna was born. I wake early to shave my balls. Not seen them without hair since the eighties. Aimee and the kids drop me at reception. I'll call when I need picking up. Registered and wrapped in a thin gown, ready, I sit and wait. Read Richard Ford from my new course reading list. No food since the night before. Stomach rumbles. An hour later than promised a nurse leads me to theatre. Local anaesthetic, then a nurse paints my balls a burnt orange. The doctor chats throughout the hour or so the procedure takes, trying and failing to take my mind off the tugs and pulls of his instruments and fingers inside my ball sack, the sensation eased but not entirely erased by the anaesthetic. His efforts manage to make the situation only a little less strangely intimate and awkward.

It's another few hours before they let me leave. When they do, I shuffle down the corridor to the cafe, only a little faster than my father managed after his last cancer op. The ache in my thighs and legs begins to blossom. I am glad to sit and order coffee and a sandwich. I phone Aimee. She will be an hour or so.

No rush, I say. I can read my book. I'll see you out front.

But she is already hanging up, the kids yanking her attention back.

Ten minutes before she is likely to arrive, I haul myself up and shuffle outside. I half sit on the short wall outside main reception. Smokers huddle away from the doors, in pyjamas and frayed slippers, artificial grey clouds hanging above them, streaking the blue sky as the breeze catches hold and wafts through.

I see the car and stand and wave. See the kids see me. Simon and Adam at the glass wave back. Smile. But the car sails past. I turn and stand and wave, both hands this time, sure that Aimee will see me in the rear-view mirror and stop. But the car continues on. Past the turning circle. Past the feed off lane for the main parking. Back into the one-way system that encircles the hospital.

I wait, but the car does not reappear. I try her mobile. Voicemail. Text: **Am outside reception. Waiting. Whr R U?**

I wait.

Nothing.

I shuffle to the pavement, look both ways for the car.

Nothing.

I am shuffling along the pavement to the parking when she sails past again. I wave. I shout. Adam and Simon are grinning through the glass. I glimpse Anna in her baby seat, howling. Still the car does not stop, but again moves past the turning circle. I shout at no one, at the once more disappearing car, as the indicator flashes and it pulls into the car park. Stops.

I shuffle to catch up. The anaesthetic has faded and each step feels like something is stabbing in my groin. Ripped stitches flash through my mind. I fume and snarl my way to the car, am ready to scream as I pull open the passenger door. They are all laughing, even Anna, who has done that toddler thing and flipped her mood like a switch.

Sorry, says Aimee. I didn't see you.

What, both times?

No, sorry. The kids said they saw you but didn't say where.

What about your phone? I sent a text.

Mummy left her phone at home, says Simon, grinning.

I saw you Daddy, says Adam. I saw you twice. I told Mummy. I saw you twice.

Aimee is laughing.

It's not funny.

It is a little bit.

She pulls the car back onto the road. I recline my seat, click the seatbelt over me, hold it loose about my waist.

You're all monsters, I say and they laugh all the more.

Aimee looks over at me. You okay?

Will be. Just take it steady, I say and nod at the road ahead.

Laid up. In bed. Painkillers and cups of tea. The kids come and sit beside me. They are careful not to jog me. Adam curls up that afternoon and sleeps beside me. Aimee brings me toast and sandwiches. Anna toddles round the double bed, grinning, unable to clamber up onto the mattress but she keeps trying all the same.

Later, noise from downstairs. The clatter of plates and cutlery, the clunk of pots and pans. Aimee brings me a plate up and I eat and listen to them, all four of them at the kitchen table. This is all of us. At least until one of the kids makes grandparents of us. This is the family we are. Complete.

I expect him to appear. To say something. But I eat alone, a book propped on the pillow beside me and I listen to them downstairs. There is laughing. Simon asks about desert. Aimee calls up to me, asks if I want some.

*

Half-asleep. A Saturday morning in September. Just months after our wedding. Sounds from the bathroom: clattering; the clang of the pedal bin lid; the shush and shish of Aimee peeing. I know it's her because there's only us in the house. This is before kids, before any of the kids. I stretch on the bed, blink at the sun creeping under the curtains of the bedroom of our first home together. I hear the toilet flush and I hear Aimee call out, hear her cry.

She runs back into the bedroom, throws herself onto the bed, her face and voice a mush of tears. I don't know what's wrong until I see the pregnancy test in her hand. I usher her in next to me, do my best to calm her.

It's okay, we can keep trying. We knew it might take a little time. Can't expect it to work first time. It's only been a month since we ditched the contraception. It's still early days.

No, she blurts between sobs, No. You don't understand.

She holds out the stick, waves it at me. A blue line crosses the little window. By the time we have finish having kids, the tests move from blue lines and plus signs to displaying the word Pregnant in clean type.

We're going to have a baby, she says.

I wrap her in my arms. We hold each other.

Shit, I say. Then, That's brilliant. That's wonderful.

The first time I see him is as I hurry along the ancient, almost subterranean central corridor back to Salisbury Hospital's maternity wards, desperately wishing that everything will be okay. I want him then. Want a quick word, a hug, a hand on my shoulder. Anything. But he has been dead two years now. Where did that go? Two years. I no longer think of him every day, not consciously. He hangs in the corner of my eye sometimes, the corner of a thought. And sometimes a song will make the loss of him tangible for a minute of two. Carry the grief back on a lyric or a sweep of melody.

But right now, walking this interminable corridor, I chant in time to my echoing footsteps.

Please let them both be okay. Please let it all be okay. Please. Please.

I don't believe in God, so who am I talking to?

I wish you were here.

I speak the words without thinking. Repeat them.

I wish you were here.

And answer my own question twice over.

I'm about to step into theatre and hold Aimee's hand through whatever is about to happen; about to watch my baby fight his way into the world; about to be the first person to wrap arms around the tiny bundle of life that he is; about to become a father, though surely I have been a father since before now; since the first time I felt his fist push against the taught dome of Aimee's belly; since listening to him hiccup, my head pressed to Aimee's skin, listening, listening, listening; since watching him on a monitor screen at 20 weeks, at 10 weeks; since listening to his heartbeat through a crackling speaker time after time; since a bright Saturday in September and the words, We're going to have a baby. Truth is, I became a father when I wasn't paying attention and now the person I most want to see before stepping into that room is my father. I want my dad.

As if wanting is enough to make it so, he appears at the

end of the corridor, holds the double doors open. My steps quicken. At the door I do not speak. Nor does he. No time to waste. My wife and child are waiting.

I step through the doors, feel his hand on my shoulder. The doors clatter closed behind me. I don't look back. I know he is gone.

Paddy & K'Den

Toby Litt

THE DEAN CAME INTO PADDY'S OFFICE, AFTER KNOCKING, and went straight for the shelves behind Paddy's chair – the location of what were later to be known as 'the offending articles'.

'Right,' said the Dean, awkwardly. She was looking at Paddy's half-ironic collection of Max's discarded and no-longer-loved figurines. They were not where, one by one, over the years, Paddy had placed them – which was on the shelf in front of his Heideggers, equidistant from each other by about three centimetres.

They had been placed, instead, he now saw, into meaningful positions of sex. The green plastic soldier, with no head, appeared to be fucking a goofily smiling pink-haired troll up the arse. Lego Yoda's head was between the legs of a Power Ranger with a piece of curled wire instead of a left foot. Worst of all, one of those jelly monsters with a big mouth of badly painted teeth was going down on a bald Playmobil air-hostess whose hair – Paddy remembered – had fallen down a hole in the living room floorboards.

'My son,' said Paddy, 'and his best friend.'

'Yes,' said the Dean. She was a tired woman of sixty-five who specialized in the Icelandic Sagas.

'Half term,' said Paddy. 'They were in here by themselves for, what, six or seven minutes. I had to do some photocopying.'

'Right.'

'I didn't put these like this,' said Paddy. 'Why would I?'

'The student alleges that throughout the tutorial in question you kept repeatedly referring to Heidegger, as if to force her attention to *that shelf.*'

The layout of the room was such that two uncomfortable oatmeal-coloured and -textured armchairs faced one another beside the door. Paddy always sat on the one with his back to his desk, and his shelves running to the vanishing point behind his left elbow. The student, whoever they were, sat facing him. This meant that the plastic figures were somewhere behind his head – always in view.

'But that's ludicrous,' said Paddy, and wished he'd said *absurd*, because *ludicrous* sounded too middle-class and flippant. He knew the trouble he was in was serious.

'I believe you,' said the Dean. 'I don't think it something you would do.'

'Why would I leave them there, like *that*?'

'I believe you are due to see the student in half an hour. She is very distressed.'

'So you think I just set them up, just now?'

'No, no, no,' said the Dean. Paddy was relieved. 'But it's *proving* that you didn't.'

'Why do I have to *prove*? I just said I didn't.'

'I'm afraid it's your word against hers.' The clichés of officialdom.

Paddy knew the student. Fatima. She didn't like him; he didn't give her high enough grades. There was nothing he could say to get through to her or change her, until she failed.

She was a foreign student; her fees were high. Philosophy was an excuse, as far as he could see, for her to live in London and to shop for nailcare products.

'Oh fuck.'

Paddy moved toward the shelf to de-arrange the toys.

'No!' shouted the Dean. 'Sorry, no. We'll have to take some images of that, for reference.' She hadn't said *evidence*.

Paddy had been wondering why the Dean was holding a copy of the *Daily Telegraph*. Now the Dean, with her iPad, took lots of photos of the toys, with the paper included in the foreground to confirm the date. Like a hostage video.

'What can I do?' asked Paddy.

'I suppose we'll have to talk to your son and his friend.'

'K'Den,' said Paddy, then spelled it. 'He's black. Well, sort of mixed race.'

'I don't see what bearing that has,' said the Dean.

'I was explaining the weird spelling.'

'Weird is subjective,' said the Dean.

'Well, have you ever met anyone called K-apostrophe-D-E-N? Have you?'

'I haven't met a lot of people, Paddy,' said the Dean. 'That doesn't mean they're weird.'

Paddy was becoming angrier.

'Are you seriously suggesting that I get turned on by putting *those* like *that* before a female student comes in?'

'Those are your words, Paddy, not mine. I hope we can sort this out as speedily as possible. Where are your son and K'Den now?'

'At school,' said Paddy, and gave the name.

'That's not too far,' said the Dean. 'I was due at an HEFCE meeting today, but…'

'What?'

'I will have to go and speak to them – and you can't have any contact with Max beforehand.'

'This student,' said Paddy. 'She's angry at me. I've told her she's going to fail, and she's doing this to get at me. She's not really offended by that.'

'We have to be seen to take this accusation with the utmost seriousness, Paddy.'

'She's just using her religion.'

'You are the first person to mention her religion,' said the Dean.

This stalled Paddy. He knew he should shut up. 'Can I put them back now?' he said, meaning the toys.

'I suppose so,' said the Dean, after checking the image was on her iPad and, simultaneously, being uploaded to the Cloud.

*

Paddy was taken to H.R., where he had to wait. His phone was confiscated, although the phrase used was 'we'll just shoosh it over to this little drawer over in my desk, okay?' From one of the office phones, he called the school to let them know the Dean was coming.

'She needs to ask Max some questions,' Paddy said to the woman in the school office, the nice one who smiled all the time. He managed to stop himself saying, 'It's not about child abuse – I am not an abusive father.'

The H.R. people, some of whom he had met before, and disliked, kept offering him cups of tea, telling him it would all be alright, and then going off to gossip about him.

Paddy read a copy of *Hello* magazine, twice.

The Dean returned about half past five in the evening.

'Bad news, I'm afraid,' she said. She looked more tired than Paddy had ever seen her. 'Both boys deny doing anything.'

'Of course they do,' said Paddy. 'They were terrified of what would happen to them.'

'No leading questions were asked.'

'But what did you say? You took them out of the classroom, I hope.'

'Yes. We did. The female police officer – '

'Oh Christ,' said Paddy.

'Well, they're going to think I'm covering my back if I back you up,' said the Dean.

'Can I phone Agatha now, and explain why I'm not home yet?'

'Before you do that, I need to get your side of the story straight.'

'Can I at least text?'

'This is very serious, Paddy. You're being accused of sexually grooming this young woman.'

Paddy laughed, and realized that was the worst thing he could do. He had seen enough films about the downfall of arrogant white men.

Soberly, too soberly, he said, 'I will answer any questions I need to.'

'Would you like a cup of tea?' asked the Dean.

*

When Paddy arrived home, around ten, Agatha said, 'I know.'

K'Den's mother had phoned her after school, and then Agatha had called one of Paddy's work colleagues – who'd said, 'Shouldn't tell you this,' then told her.

Paddy said, 'I want to speak to Max.'

'He's asleep,' said Agatha. 'He was very upset. He thought the Policeman had come to arrest him.'

'It was a woman.'

'He told me there were two of them.'

'What a waste of time,' said Paddy. 'Did he say what happened? Has he confessed to you?'

'No, Max said he didn't do anything wrong.'

'I think he probably didn't,' said Paddy. 'It's K'Den, that evil little so-and-so. I'm sure his Dad lets him watch anything on the internet he likes. He's got an iPad, he stays up till all hours.'

'So K'Den's suddenly the devil,' said Agatha.

'Yes,' Paddy said. 'He's had a bad effect on that class ever since he arrived. I've never liked him being friends with Max.'

'You've never particularly liked *any* of Max's friends.'

Paddy was making himself a peanut butter bagel as they talked.

'Are you going to be a bit more supportive? Look…' and Paddy gave his account of events.

'No, I don't think you'd do that,' Agatha said after hearing it all through from the Dean's arrival to Paddy's 'release from H.R.'

'Whatever Max says now, even if he changes his story, they won't believe it,' Paddy said. 'They'll think he's been pressured by me.'

'Do you think you'll lose your job?'

'If they don't believe me.'

'She's just a student.'

'She's a rich, spoiled, angry Muslim female student who

has bright purple fingernails, wears high heels and a push-up bra and a scarf on the very back of her head and enough perfume to make you gag. I'm fucked.'

Agatha cradled Paddy's head.

'What day did Max come to your office?'

'The 16th. Half term. Wednesday.'

'So that's two weeks – two weeks one day.'

'Yes.'

'And no-one noticed anything? Not even what Yoda was up to?'

'It's not funny.'

'What's going to happen now?'

Paddy stepped out of Agatha's arms, and explained about the investigation. His other students were all going to be asked, discreetly, if they had noticed anything unusual in his office.

He finished the bagel.

*

The next morning, Paddy tried to be loving towards Max, and not angry. He said nothing as Max ate Nutella on toast, something he was only usually allowed at the weekend or during the holidays.

But after Max had brushed his teeth, been helped into his schooliform (sweatshirt, sweatpants and bright yellow football trainers) and had his hair brushed, Paddy needed to ask.

'Daddy's in trouble,' he said. 'I have to know if you put those things on the shelf in my office into sexy positions.'

Max laughed.

'You said 'saxy', he said.

'Sexy,' said Paddy.

'Sexy,' said Max. It was just as funny.

'What do you know about it?' Paddy asked. 'About sex.'

Agatha, who had been standing on the stairs, said, 'Be a bit less weird, okay?' She turned to Max. 'We just need to know if you arranged those things to look like they were doing things to each other. For a joke.'

'I didn't,' said Max.

'You didn't,' said Paddy. 'Okay. Did anyone else?'

'No,' said Max.

'You weren't in there on your own. And I won't blame you,' said Paddy. 'But did K'Den do it?'

'No-one did it,' said Max. 'You did it.'

'He won't get in trouble,' Paddy said. 'He was just doing something funny. He probably thought it was a good joke.'

Paddy – not sleeping the whole night – had remembered the boys laughing when he re-entered the room, the warm photocopied pages in his hand. He'd thought it was something they'd found in his office. Some sweets eaten from his desk. He couldn't understand how he hadn't noticed the toys on the shelf, and their changed positions.

'I'll take him to school,' Paddy said.

*

They drove with a dance radio station playing. Paddy couldn't help noticing how sex-obsessed all the lyrics were. Extended metaphors for blow jobs. He didn't turn it off, though. It was Max's favourite.

The woman in the school office was very bright, and

called him Mr.

Max's teacher, Miss Samson, asked if he was okay. He, Paddy.

'Could I have a word?' Paddy asked.

Outside, in the hall where assemblies featuring numbers, letters and fairy tales took place, Paddy said, 'Have you noticed anything about K'Den? Any over-sexualized behaviour?'

Miss Samson looked over Paddy's shoulder. 'That wouldn't be appropriate,' she said. She nodded, and Paddy understood. He'd hoped to have a little more time.

When he turned around, he saw K'Den with his mother on his left and his father on his right. The father was black, the mother mostly white.

'I don't like the Police talking to my son,' said K'Den's father. He was shorter than Paddy but a lot more muscular. For some reason, Paddy had always imagined him in bad fancy-dress, as a pirate in ripped polyester clothes. K'Den's mother had a ludicrous blonde wig and such long fingernails that, when she came round one afternoon after school, she'd dropped and smashed Agatha's favourite coffee cup. Her name was Daisy. The father's name was Sammy.

'I don't like being accused of things I haven't done,' said Paddy.

The Head Teacher was already there between them. Where had she been hiding? Clearly, Paddy thought, this scene had been anticipated.

'Hello,' he said. 'I would like K'Den moved to another class. I don't want him in the same class as Max.'

'I think we should discuss this in my office,' said the Head Teacher.

'Oh, *really?*' said Sammy.

The Head Teacher was a very tall woman with orange hair and bright yellow fingernails.

'And why not?' asked Daisy.

'Because he's a corrupting influence,' said Paddy, then ducked back. He'd thought Sammy was going to hit him, but the father was only turning to Daisy and laughing.

Paddy knew he sounded like he was from the 1950s.

Quite a few of the children from Max's class were gathered in the doorway, watching. K'Den was among them, Max wasn't.

'Let's go, shall we?' said the Head Teacher.

*

Paddy went first. In her office, looking at a yellow Lever-Arch file on the shelves labelled Racist Incidents, Paddy told her what he thought of K'Den and K'Den's parents.

The Head Teacher listened, nodded, made sympathetic noises and said she understood his position.

'But do you agree?' asked Paddy.

'Even if I did,' said the Head Teacher. 'I couldn't say. But as it happens, I don't.'

Paddy really wanted to rip apart the illogic of those two statements. But he knew it wouldn't help.

As he went out, he passed Sammy and Daisy.

'I know what your house is like,' he said. 'Every time Max came home having learned a new bad word, it came from your son.'

'That's enough,' said the Head.

'You buy him every violent video game, so Max begs for them. Your son drinks caffeinated drinks –'

'Enough!'

Sammy was smirking, arms crossed.

'– until midnight, then is a disinterested zombie all the next day, who thinks school is crap because it doesn't involve killing.'

The Head Teacher was pushing at Paddy, to get him to leave.

'Miss Farrell knows it's true, even though she can't say – but boys like yours make her job much harder. I'm leaving. Let go. I'm leaving.'

*

Paddy walked twice along the sea-front, ashamed of himself, phoned the Head to apologize, then went home and tried to do some reading. He couldn't, so he went out walking again.

*

When Max got home from school he said, 'I hate you – you're the worst Dad, ever – you made everyone hate me.'

*

The Dean phoned on Monday afternoon to say the inquiry had been inconclusive.

None of Paddy's students could remember whether the toys were in sexualized positions or not.

'So I'm okay – for the moment,' asked Paddy.

'The student is prepared to compromise. If you apologize, and aren't allowed to have one-on-one tutorials with female students in the future.'

'No,' said Paddy. 'Everyone will think I did it.'

'Now this has taken a lot of work and negotiation, Paddy. If you agree, it'll be over. Everyone will eventually forget.'

'They won't and I can't,' said Paddy. 'My students need to trust me.'

'They all backed you up. You'd never said or done anything inappropriate. None of them had ever felt awkward in your presence.'

'That's a lie,' said Paddy. 'They all feel awkward. They're children, and I know something they don't, and they hate it.'

'I'll let you think about it,' the Dean said. 'You can give me an answer tomorrow. We have one or two more students left to talk to.'

'Who?' Paddy asked, hoping for one at least who occasionally lifted their eyes from the floor.

'I can't say. But you never know, they may help.'

*

With feelings that he might soon be reduced to a house husband, Paddy spent that evening trying to get back as friends with Max. He kept off from mentioning K'Den, and listened as hard as he could to the statistics from Max's Match Attax cards.

During the day, Paddy had gone to the Post Office and bought five packs – as a craven, obvious attempt to force a hug. It had worked, but Max was very unnatural as he inspected the fresh cards. His manner reminded Paddy of how he'd been after his arm was broken – Daddy's fault – a few years before. The thought that Max was wincing away from him, physically or psychologically, tore at Paddy. He had expected rejection in angry adolescence, not so early as this.

*

Agatha, in bed, was more loving. They kissed and she said she believed him completely. K'Den *was* a bad influence, she admitted. But there was always going to be The One Boy, she said, in any class. The One Boy the others idolize.

'But why does he always have to be such a slimy little shit,' asked Paddy, and it was a real question. He didn't understand how the world worked, or what people liked. When he saw r'n'b videos, he could tell the young men were slimy little shits, flagrantly insincere. Why couldn't everyone else tell? All *I love you forever baby*, and the women believed it, but only *I love you forever baby* until you give it up, then I'm out of here and off to the next sleazy seduction, probably using the exact same words. The whole culture seemed to be based around preening little toerags, plucked eyebrows and affectedly shaved heads, who told you it was okay to use and abuse bitches and ho's.

This was who Max would end up wanting to be, if he didn't become an indie kid. Faux-black. And he'd never have the same cultural capital as someone like K'Den. He would waste years trying to get in with boys who, ultimately, would hold him in contempt. He said something like this to Agatha, who said, 'Perhaps that's what Max needs. We can't tell him who to be friends with. It just won't work. And if we warn him off, it'll work against us.'

'I know you're right,' said Paddy. 'But that fucking Pharrell with his fucking 'Happy'.'

It was the wrong reference; Paddy was too exhausted to correct it.

*

On Tuesday, he took the car to be serviced and on Wednesday he put up a shelf in Max's room that was only a little not-straight and on Thursday he was exonerated.

'You're lucky to have such technologically advanced students,' said the Dean, who'd had her secretary call Paddy in for a twelve o'clock meeting.

Paddy was smartly dressed for his sacking, and had gone to the corner shop to beg for some cardboard boxes to begin emptying his office.

'Stop pissing around,' said Paddy. 'Tell me.'

'Your student from Norway,' the Dean said, ignoring the swearing. 'Christina Olofsdottor.'

'Yes,' said Paddy. 'She remembered?'

'The offending articles,' they had become that now, 'are behind your chair,' said the Dean. 'You Skype her. She records you. But what's really lucky is – we have once a week for the last three weeks. We have the day after the day you claim – '

Paddy didn't hear any more than snatches from now on. His heart was migrating around his body. Sometimes it was in his right ear, sometimes in his throat, sometimes his gut.

The Dean showed Christina Olofsdottir's screenshots. His face. His shelves. A date PowerPointed above them.

In one of them, he'd got up to fetch a book and left the webcam an unobstructed view. It was the week after half term – the toys were still giving one another too good a time. Paddy *hadn't* un-posed and re-posed them, specifically for the purposes of grooming an attractive, vulnerable female Muslim student. She'd made her case too strongly – she couldn't scale back. Someone else would take over tutoring her – a female colleague. Paddy wouldn't be involved in assessing her work. Paddy could resume teaching next week. It might be an idea, however, if the figures were removed. The Dean finished speaking.

'Fuck,' said Paddy.

'If our good Nordic friend hadn't recorded your tutorials, you would still be in serious trouble,' said the Dean, smiling.

Paddy thought of Christina Olofsdottor and her white, so white, screenlit face.

'I *did* believe you, you know. You're not like that.'

Sound Boys

Courttia Newland

Paps always told me records were marked with the weight of time. He said trapped sounds and words released memories that lasted long after the music faded into a hiss of empty space. He taught me to respect their power, to treasure every vinyl in my collection, no matter how warped or scratched. To this day, I won't part with a single record. I doubt I ever will.

On Paps' birthday, mum plays a selection of his favourite tunes. The Wailers, Alton Ellis, Big Youth, Toots and The Maytals, Sugar Minott, Gregory Issacs and Dennis Brown. The furtive bass makes our walls murmur in baritone and can be heard three houses away. Most of the records are seven inch discs, black like dilated pupils, warped humps that make the needle bounce, never skip. Over time I've grown used to the annual gathering of blank-faced elders wearing dull suits and dresses, holding white plastic cups that scrunch whenever they make a point. Mum's old kitchen becomes filled with that brittle language, as though the cups are bored with our company, and have decided to talk with the walls instead.

Back when my Paps was doling out sermons on the fervent religion of our culture, and I was aged 8 or 9, I can't quite remember, the energy of those gatherings was ecstatic. For a full week before my parents threw a function there was the dry, sinus-loosening smell of marinating goat, minced lamb, the damp, green seasoning pushed deep into the crevices of assorted chicken pieces; the fine dust of flour that created dumplings, patties, roti. Come the weekend my mother and father woke early, and while I played in the garden there came the rhythmic click of the gas hob lighting, dials turned to fire up the oven. Cooking smells rose, saturating the air. Hunger clawed at my belly while I tried to concentrate on my Evel Knievel's wind up stunts. Paps would play hissing Coxsone tapes, or recordings of Rodigan on Capital Radio. When I ventured into the kitchen I found bubbling pots, sizzling pans, steam that would float like some ancient ancestral spirit. I cried for a taste of something, anything.

Towards late afternoon, as the sun fell from the sky, Paps would disappear into the living room. Music began to bleed from his custom built, wardrobe-sized speakers. Later that night, the house filled with a stream of well-dressed men and women until it swelled and felt as though it might burst. The lights dimmed into darkness, and there was only music, the chatter of appreciation and the shuffle of feet on old battered floorboards. The kitchen became an island of light, food, and adult company, where I could perhaps find other kids, the comforting hug of a family friend, or dumplings filled with warm, spicy meat.

A few words on my parents; my mother, the perfect mix of fragility and strength, four foot eleven and a half, the only girl of seven boys. I see her now, that young, thin-lipped expression forever bordered on disgust, the black halo of hair, bright lips and slightly protruding teeth, dishing out food, stepping steady from foot to foot, moving to the rhythm;

and again, when some man tried to get fresh, grabbing her from behind and winding against her, the speed of the hot metal ladle as it lashed his face; him falling, my mother stood over his tall frame and cussing fast. A girlish woman, apart from her tomboy insistence on climbing trees, and fighting, playing football and cricket with the men, and the fact she rarely smiled, yet still I felt loved and protected, as did my father. Her firm stance, legs slightly apart grounding her as sure as electricity pylons, her broad yet tiny feet, her joyful dance, her quiet determination. Her impeccable, buttoned up professionalism when she left home for her job as a nursery school teacher, hardly recognisable to me, her disbelieving son.

And him; the smiling, skanking, slow bouncing, smoke trailing, sweet-rum-smelling, always ready to ramp figure of a man alongside his nocturnal alter ego. The dark father poised behind twin turntables, the huge shadow looming behind the low wall of the sound system, controlling the crowd of people whether squeezed into our living room or packed into a hall of thousands; make them bawl 'murder!', or Paps' name, or those of the MCs who chanted beside him, either Mellow Man or Rankin D, long arms and legs and locks shooting out like disco lights, the darkness a warm cocoon that called me from the kitchen, desperate to feel immersed.

I'd squeeze along the passageway, cramped by people, into a forest of shuffling legs, pushing until I reached the low wall, where Mellow Man would prop a spliff in the corner of his mouth, lift me over the partition, into the secluded nest of the sound area. Dad smiled, often placed a hand on my head and let me sit awhile, surrounded by circular twelves, sevens and tens. I loved the coloured wax best, the blood reds, sunset oranges, and bright electric blues. Sometimes he'd even play what I held high. From that vantage point I saw the dance in a light of the privileged few. It was another world, one of knobs and dials and sliders and record boxes, and what happened next was inevitable I suppose. As I watched the men grip the mic and chant over the blank canvas of crowd, I murmured beneath my breath, head low, imitating their cadence and words. This continued throughout the week, inside the loneliness of my slim bedroom, in the school playground, and the back seat of Paps' car as he played sound tapes, incantations becoming imprinted on my brain. It didn't take long for me to improvise my own lyrics, and devise these into my own songs.

Once, as I stood behind the turntables, Rankin D passed me the mic by mistake. I took it before he could pull away, and started to talk as the crowd laughed at the pitch of my voice, began to chant as they bawled out loud in amazement, which soon became encouragement, and it was done. They let me have it, as I made the crowd rock. The slapping of palms and the tight, eternal hug Paps gave me when I'd finished were the warmest I'd ever known.

That did it. Every few weekends I was allowed to venture into the night with Paps when he played out, even though my mum didn't wholeheartedly approve. I don't know how he convinced her, but I was grateful.

Still, those were different times. When adults thought nothing of leaving their kids locked in cars while they had a swift pint in the pub with their mates after cricket; when we used pocket money to buy packs of candy cigarettes, complete with dusted red tips, pretending to smoke before we ate them in swift bites. When our parents allowed us to jump on rusting Choppers, or in my case a Striker, to ride as far around our neighbourhood as we liked, totally unsupervised. At 10 years of age I had kissed girls, drunk beer, fought boys and run. This was the late Seventies, bordering early Eighties. We knew nothing but this.

On that particular Saturday I prepared myself even more than usual. I had on a pair of Nike Bruins, white with a blue swoosh; blue Farahs, a white Pierre Cardin shirt, and a brand new leather jacket fresh with the scent of originality. Paps wore a similar white shirt, a beige flat cap, and his slacks were a matching camel brown, the crease sharp as the tips of his gleaming leather shoes. The thin gold chain around his neck caught the rheumy bedroom light, hanging low inside his shirt. He surveyed what I was wearing down to my socks, just to make sure I was good enough to step out with him. We dressed together in his bedroom so he could keep an eye on me I reckon, and when we were ready, we stood with our heads close, posing before the mirror. Seeing what we liked, we slapped palms and snapped fingers. Mum lay on the bed in her dressing gown, reading one of her books, trying not to smile.

We were headed north, to Stokey. Paps' sound, Bagga Wire, was due to clash with Virgo, a local crew. That evening brought castor sugar frost and a light blue van parked outside our house, driven by Lizard, Paps' best friend from JA, and his Chief Operator/Selector. Lizard pretty much looked like his nick-name; bulging green eyes, thin neck and ping pong ball of an Adam's apple; tall and slim to the point of starvation, except his size was deceiving; he ate every opportunity, one of the reasons he loved our house mum always said. Lizard was the Bagga Wire crew member I most admired. He was funny and laid back, smooth with the ladies and charming with kids.

I called him Uncle and he called me Nephew for most of our lives; that even became my Dee Jay name; Natty Nephew.

There were others in the sound; Mercy and Armour, the Box Boys, Mellow Man and Rankin D, the MCs, Bookie the technician, and my father, known as Paps Dekka J (number One Selector, usually shortened to Paps DJ). Although the others were well mannered, talented and hard-working, they didn't like kids as much as Lizard, so I don't remember them as well.

At that stage of the evening, which occurred practically every Saturday for the first 11 years of my life, the routine was always the same. The blue van would pull up outside my living room window. I'd rush to the front door to let them in. They'd troop into the house, loud and tall, producing peals of ear-shattering laughter, to talk with Mum and Paps for about half an hour, drinking Guinness, white rum, or tea. They moved the sound equipment; speaker boxes, pre and valve amps, echo chambers, turntables, mixing desk, endless boxes of records, microphones, metres of cables and much, much more; carrying them all into the van, bit by complicated bit, until the living room was as bare and empty as a derelict house. Mum co-ordinated like a general. I'd help as much as I could, carrying seven inch boxes, or microphones. On this occasion, when the room was empty, I kissed Mum and ran out of the front door, to climb beside Paps in the passenger seat. Lizard touched my chin lightly with his fist. The van side door slid shut and the engine turned over, shuddering beneath my scarred and wounded seat, and we were off into the London night.

The journey; a haze of dub tapes and ganja smoke, aluminium containers of steaming rice and peas, tanned bottles of stout, the pungent smell of Old Spice. The city unfurling through the wide windscreen like a live action movie, or so it seemed to my young eyes. I'm not sure if I was high from second hand inhalation, or unused to being up so late; most dances didn't start until after 10, so we arrived at the venue around 9, and although excitement always managed to keep me awake at home, as soon as I lay back on the soft imitation leather, my eyes would close and I'd fall asleep, hypnotised by the glittering, swinging, red, gold and green Lion of Judah Lizard hung from the rear view mirror. In what seemed like a moment, I'd feel the van decelerate. We'd pull up outside the venue. That night it was a community hall on a Stoke Newington estate, brimming with people bubbling to bass heavy tunes that rattled from a fish grey Mark 3 Ford Capri, up on the curb, twin doors wide open.

I helped Mercy and Armour unload the equipment on Paps' chosen end of the hall, and then it was time to string up. This was Bookie's main area of expertise (besides drinking, smoking, and digging out yam and potato, he always assured– years passed before I understood what he meant). At that early stage of the night, Bookie became the sound system's corporal, under the watchful eye of my Paps. I'd wander around, trying to lend a hand by locating a screwdriver, or carefully passing a red hot soldering iron, while Bookie reconnected loose wiring, or replaced the blown fuses of Paps' beloved Quads.

Following that came my second favourite part of the night: The Sound Check, heralded by the bass thud of the power switch as it was turned on. Without fail, Paps always played his favourite dub for the test; a Sugar Minott ode to the Bagga Wire sound system Paps had travelled over 4 thousand miles to record himself. Tweeters played alone, the sharp treble setting my teeth on edge; then mid-range, and then the two were brought together, so those gathered and working inside the hall could finally hear Minott's soaring voice echo over the empty hall. Either Mellow Man or Rankin D tested the microphone, with a 'Mic *check*, Mic *check*... Ch, ch, *check*... *One*, one, one...' If I was lucky, I could have a turn. When Paps was happy everything sounded criss, he turned a dial and pulsing bass rocked the hall. Mercy and Armour worked fast securing any trailing wires. Paps turned the dub plate down so that Virgo, stacking a tower of speaker boxes and amps on the opposite end of the hall, could run their own equipment check.

I made myself busy being a child; hanging around the bustling kitchen until I got under everyone's feet, and was given a saltfish patty and sent away; climbing skeletal frames on the monochrome estate playground with random kids, either the sons and daughters of box boys or ravers; playing by myself, wandering the upstairs rooms of the hall, the committee rooms, offices and library; but I often found that frightening, and came back down. I tried to stay away from the sound in that brief hiatus before the people began to arrive, because that was mainly when I was made to run chores. If I timed it right, after the first two or three tunes and the men were in full flow, they'd be too focused on the music and the crowd to see me as anything but what I saw in myself; a secret weapon in their arsenal that would bury Virgo.

That night I timed it perfectly. By the time I made my appearance Paps was jamming hard, one hand on the mixer, the other on his echo chamber, eyes on the crowd as his waist moved and he bit his lower lip in concentration. Lizard leant over a speaker box, crumbling dark substance onto white paper. The others rocked by themselves as Mellow Man took his usual role warming up the mic. After a few more dubs, Rankin D stepped forward, and the MCs upped the pace; trading lyrics, passing the mic back and forth between them. When they said anything too lewd, Lizard reached over and covered my ears, but I always wriggled away. 'Yuh too bad mind,' he told me. Paps' mouth was a thin line but his eyes crinkled at the sides. I tried to ignore both and look mature.

The two MCs chanted the crowd to fever pitch. I listened, rocked and swayed and then it was my turn. I don't remember much except thin perspiration on my temples, the roar of the crowd and the dub Paps spun to accompany my lyrics, a tune that has stayed imprinted in my mind forever. Whatever I said that night is lost, unless someone has a recording of that clash. Something about school, being as good on the mic as any man, how suave I was with the ladies and lots about my age. I know a tape of that clash must have existed, but I searched Paps' collection for years and never found it. Maybe he'd destroyed it. I've tried to find the recording ever since, yet there's nothing on CD, YouTube, or cassette. Bagga Wire vs Virgo, Bloomfield community centre, Stoke Newington, 1981. If anyone has information, I'd be grateful if they passed it on.

The crowd of people made the walls shake with noise when I put the microphone down. There were the usual slapped palms and hugs from various Bagga Wire members, which I took in my stride. Paps had a strategy that worked well for the previous clashes where I'd performed; he timed my appearance last, so it was me, Natty Nephew, who stuck out in the crowd's mind when they decided who'd win. As I was lifted up under my armpits and held over the turntables, their whistles, roars and shouts became frenzied, almost wild.

Lizard lifted me even higher, until I was sat on his shoulders, and bounced on his toes so the crowd could see me even at the back. The roars grew even louder. From where I was sitting, I could see the Virgo sound men rapidly throwing on a dub, cueing up the record. They'd panicked. I had made them panic. I pumped my fist in the air, yelling victory over Lizard's head, my cries drowned by the strength of the people before me.

I saw him. The young boy, moving from the back of the set and the thick knot of people, pushing forwards, grabbing the microphone quick, as though he'd stolen it. He seemed nervous, but he looked right at me. He was taller than me, older; I guessed 13. He wore a black beanie and a red Sergio Tucchini tracksuit, and had a thin gold chain. One of the Virgo MCs introduced him as Styla Dan, and then without any pause, still looking across the mass of people into my eyes, the youth started to chant.

It was mesmerising. The dub Virgo dropped rattled with sub bass that I could feel in my rib cage and teeth; my ears rang with deep vibrations and the men in the crowd began to throw their washcloths into the air; the hall became a mass of spinning, turning colours, reds, blues, browns, whites and yellows, like miniature kites. I felt Lizard's shoulders stiffen beneath me. Styla only managed to chant his chorus twice, and a section of intro before the people began to grow so rowdy, the selector had to pull the record back. While the MC talked into the silence, and kept the crowd waiting for the right amount of time before the selector dropped needle onto the wax again, Styla bit his lip, his eyes fixed on me, an ebony statue in the darkness, black and strong. I couldn't hold it. His gaze was too intense. I turned to face the men gathered beneath me, and was amazed to see them staring at the dusty floor, or their feet. They wouldn't look at me. I couldn't believe it. Was it so obvious? Was he that better? Was I so young?

I spun around, probably hurting Lizard quite a bit, to see what my Paps made of this unexpected Virgo move. He was motionless, hands by his side, paler than I had ever seen him, and he was biting his lower lip, nervous, almost chewing on his own flesh. He lowered his eyes from mine too, but before that there was something as haunting as the community hall's empty rooms. And then I saw it. I spun back to face Styla, and he was doing the same. Biting his lip, almost chewing. It was difficult to see in the shadows, but I was struck by a sense of childish intuition that broked no hesitation, or second guessing; it *felt* right, so I decided, so it was. Styla Dan resembled Paps. It was too close to be coincidence. As the sub bass and steady drums began to resound, I slipped from Lizard's shoulders to the concrete floor. As the hands reached out to grab me, I slipped between them and away, snaking around speaker stacks, pushing onto the dancefloor and the immense gathering of people, and then I was small enough to duck and escape, moving fast across the expanse of hall, and although they could see the trail of people part as I went, they couldn't move as fast as I, and as it was Styla Dan's turn to MC, they couldn't disrespect Virgo by giving chase.

I forced my way to the centre of the men and women, immersed in sweat and smoke, closer to the Virgo speakers, piled monoliths on either side of the set, bass gods. I watched Styla Dan chant lyrics in a deep, confident and assured baritone I could never match. His flow was natural, his subject matter relevant, and he had lived life far more vibrantly than I, mature though I thought I was. Once I was closer, it was easy to see. I had made the crowd rock. Styla destroyed their senses and put them back together, made anew. The selector switched to another, deadlier dubplate, said; 'Pure bass ya now,' let it drop. A wave of devastation. I could feel the warm breeze of deep bass notes on my cheeks like a fresh summer day. Styla launched into a new lyric, calmer now, swaying to the rhythm, and I was jostled on all sides by the people as they skanked and swayed. I couldn't take my eyes from him. It was all there, in his mannerism, physicality and rhythm. Everything I saw in Styla I had seen before. He was my father's son.

I ran. Back the way I had come and out of the hall, paying the shouts no heed. Out into the thick night, regardless of the cold, hearing Styla's chorus repeat in my head. My feet pattered endlessly on the concrete, or so it felt, as there was nowhere to go but where I'd already been. The ghostly construct of the estate playground, lit silver by the moon as though awash with antediluvian magic, the hard, chilled concrete and metal bars. I found a grey tube that glittered like night sky and climbed inside, avoiding the eternal puddle of water at the bottom; I put my feet up and cried. I wasn't sure exactly what hurt more; that I'd clearly lost the clash, or that I might lose Paps. In the dark of the concrete, each reason seemed as weighty and meaningful as the other. So I cried without restraint, or even a care as to whether I could be heard. Maybe I actually wanted to be.

He came, of course. Wandering the maze of metal climbing frames and see saws, slides and frost-stiffened rope pyramid. Calling my name, wandering and scared, or so it sounded. I didn't go to him, but Paps knew me well enough. It wasn't necessary. His voice got closer, and his flat tapered shoes appeared by the bright hole of the tube. There was no reason to stay. I climbed, teeth chattering, into the moonlight.

I'd been tricked; at first I stood, head bowed, angry and ashamed, contemplating making another run. The only thing to stop me was the cold and my awareness that I was unfamiliar with the local area. Paps was equally uncomfortable, unable to face me directly, and yet nowhere as much as the beautiful woman beside him, a warm camel-coloured coat wrapped around her shoulders; which belonged to my Paps, I recognised. Next to her, was the youth. Styla Dan. His height matched hers, making them both a head taller than my father. Seeing them all look down on me, it was easy to recognise the truth no one dared to speak. And still, there was more. Their eyes told curiosity yes, but also sympathy. The woman reached out her hand. I didn't want to take it. There was betrayal in those gloved fingers, but mine were cold, and they enclosed around them despite myself, and I couldn't let go.

They were Rick and Marcy, an old friend he hadn't seen in years. Paps kept talking, and Rick watched me, and I heard what my father said in some way, but it was drowned by my thoughts, which marvelled at how much Rick's eyes resembled mine, how I had been granted something I'd secretly wished, but hadn't dared to ask for. Rick reached out his hand too. This time I took it. We stood in the centre of the playground, fingers joined.

He died two years later, before I became a teenager. Lung cancer they said, probably from all those years playing dances, inhaling vast clouds of smoke. It wasn't easy for mum, and I wouldn't like to think I've glossed over those years and the time before them, so let me speak of that; her tears in the bedroom, the thunderclap of slamming doors, her steeling herself whenever Paps left the house to travel North; the shouting and breaking glass, the months us males spent alone in the house after she left, unable to stand it. When he was diagnosed she came back without another word, and although she slept in the spare room previously filled with Paps' records, they did the best they could to raise me as husband and wife. She loved him fiercely, everyone knew it. Even after she realised he'd lied, wasn't the childless man he'd made out to be. Paps maintained he hadn't known right until the end, but I never found out the truth. Marcy wouldn't say, and Rick knew as much as I.

Now that time has come again. Paps' birthday. Mum's in the bedroom checking her emerald dress in the mirror, tying up her locks. I'm in the kitchen stirring curry goat. Marcy's rolling dumplings between her palms like a pebble while oil bubbles and trembles on the hob. Rick adds condensed milk carefully to the punch. The music plays on, and we are swaying, bathed in our silence. Sometimes it feels as though it was always this way.

Balance and Versatility

R. J. Price

'LOOK AT THOSE FIRES,' JAMES WAS SAYING TO HIS FATHER, who looked across to the clouds as well.

'They're not fires and that's not smoke.'

James let his father explain himself.

'It's dust.'

'Dust?'

Could James have known beforehand? Was it something that he might have been expected to know?

'There are huge diggers beneath those clouds – they're moving the topsoil like snow-ploughs. The earth here's so thin and dusty it smokes up like that when you move it. The diggers are making more room for more of the dump.'

No: special knowledge. He relaxed.

Now he glimpsed the diggers themselves. They were tank-tracked engines, vast; taller than two men. And yes they were in the yellow of the two snow-ploughs James knew, parked up at the depot on the outskirts of Kilellan. The Flemings passed them in the car if they were heading out for a country walk. A few minutes along that road and there was Balcraigie House, once, his mother said, a borstal, a 'school for bad boys'. Borstal is short for breaking and entering.

'They're going to run out of fields,' James looked across the flat farmland to the airport tower in the distance, 'eventually.'

His father didn't reply. He said: 'Come on, let's crack on.'

James unclicked his seatbelt and they got out of the car. The car could emergency-stop but you couldn't emergency-stop. His father had let him ride in the front where you could see outside properly. In the back you had the quarterlight's meagre triangular frame, a clamp on the world.

When would his mother allow him to sit in the front?

'Inertia belts,' your father called the seatbelts, when he'd been caught. 'Inertia belts and an air-bag.' Now, they said it when it had nothing to do with the car.

James stood still for a moment and looked towards the vast machines. 'What are they going to do with all the earth?'

'It'll end up as a football pitch. Or a motorway verge – or the garden of someone's new house. Come on.'

They moved round to the rear of the car and Mr. Fleming opened the boot. So gardens, even James's own garden, were just an extra surface on the surface of the world. They were earth but they were not the Earth.

'For the houses beyond Montgomery Avenue, maybe?' James said.

Now they were putting on their boots at the back of the car. You were allowed to say 'wellies' but you were not allowed to say 'telly'. It had something to do with his father's father.

'Maybe. Concentrate now.'

It was a hop without the hop because if you did start to move you'd lose balance and your sock would surely touch the grit.

The gulls were now flocking in scores above the vast field of rubbish. The air was thick with their cries and with the rotting smell of old vegetables, of bad metals, a bottom of the bin smell.

James looked down and saw that he was trying to put his right foot into the left boot. His big toe had worn a hole in one of the socks.

Mr. Fleming looked down at James's feet.

'Don't you ever cut your nails?'

'It's bath night tonight. Mum said –'

'Mum said, Mum said. I knew it wouldn't be your fault. Come on James, socks don't grow on trees – your big toe can see daylight through that hole. And your fingernails are just as bad!'

Socks did not grow on trees but James knew the stunted tree with cotton handkerchiefs tied on it, next to St Peter's Well. It was on one of the back-roads out towards Kilpeter, a glimpse from the car. It was something to do with single parent mothers, adoption and dead babies. Now he saw those handkerchiefs changed into socks and then the socks were Christmas stockings and his father's fishing socks at one and the same time. The clootie-tree.

He couldn't cut his nails himself. You were not to try: for instance you were not to use the black enamel kitchen scissors – a shout around the house, 'Anyone seen the black enamel kitchen scissors?' – or the secateurs (that's French).

Likewise his mother's embroidery scissors, though they were shaped and engraved to look like a Eurasian stork.

James adjusted the sock so it was looser over his toes and slipped his foot into the boot.

'Why do we have ankles, Dad?'

Mr. Fleming gripped the boot and James pushed his ankle round the pinching corner.

'Balance and versatility.'

*

'Watch out for sharp edges!'

They moved across the dump carefully, picking their way across slippery offcuts of wood, across not-quite-flattened cardboard boxes. Potato peelings filled any gaps, as if a new kind of insulation. Were potatoes all Scotland ate?

At first James held his father's hand but that made them both unstable. The piles of rubbish slid and you slid with it all, as good as an icy path. But there were can lids in the mush and folk put knives out with the rubbish thinking about anything but how they had carved the chicken. It'd be your luck your feet found a long lost blade.

Did the jewels and keys and the coins lost down the drain on Montgomery Road somehow end up here in the dump? He was keeping an eye out for a certain charm bracelet and certain five-pence pieces. There were batteries here, but they wouldn't be new.

As they moved further into the dump the bad smell began to thin. Maybe they were just getting used to it but, no, the terrain was becoming more of a proper compost heap with a richer, earthier smell. Dad had one once, and some vegetable rows, but it was all just grass now.

Flowers bloomed here. There were thick sparks of red geraniums, dark pansies. Nasturtiums trailed patch after patch of rounded leaves, a fallen clothes-line of soft greens and with flowers like scraps of duster in orange and yellow.

James slowly realised there were the blooms of household vegetables, too. There were the small white and violet petals of potato plants. There were the wide orange mouths of courgette blooms, there were the little yellow stars of straggling tomato plants in flower.

And the vegetables themselves – they seemed so solid among the paper-thin shades of flower and leaf. Marrows lying there in their own world were like large fish resting in the shadows of a river pool, waiting.

*

'This'll do,' Mr. Fleming said.

They were in the centre of the vegetable field, where tomato plants were especially prolific. The larger plants had become leggy and, weighed down with their fruit, they criss-crossed the surface of the dump. Their straggle made it easy to trip.

Mr. Fleming took a canvas bag from his shoulders and took out an identical one that had been folded inside it.

'Green ones first. Save the reds for the top.'

He stooped to pick the tomatoes and James crouched down, bottom just off the ground.

When you were down among them the tomatoes had an unclean smell. It wasn't exactly like geraniums but it was thick like geranium scent. Their stems were hairy like geraniums, too. The smell was as if the hairs were part of the atmosphere. It made him a little short of breath.

No, he did not like this tomato gathering business: he would have preferred simply to wander the dump while his father did all the work. He was a child after all and Victoria, so he'd heard, was no longer the queen.

You couldn't just snap green tomatoes off and put them in the bag: you had to hold the plant with one hand and tug and twist with the other. Before long he discovered he could take advantage of his long nails and slice quickly through the tough narrow stem that held each fruit to its parent. The sap stained his fingers with a sticky yellowish-greenish colour and a mushy pulp clogged his nails.

Mum and Dad would just have to suffer it.

Gradually he began to complete the first layer in his bag.

His father was much quicker. Soon, exhausting the tomato plants close by, he was wandering further and further away. James noticed he had produced another canvas bag from the first one, having filled the original in minutes. 'Thought this might come in handy,' he had said to himself, sounding almost guilty.

*

James looked into his own bag and judged it perhaps half full (which is the same as 50%). He thought it was time to start picking the ripened tomatoes.

There were not many of them on any one plant and James changed from crouching in the green funk to striding from plant to plant. He moved further and further into the dump. Maybe he'd get close enough to the airport to see an aircraft land. You only saw the undercarriage if you were close. He thought of the thick clutch of wheels in a plane's undercarriage as a sprig of round dark tomatoes.

His father was a distant figure behind him now. When you looked back sometimes he was obscured by squalls of dust sent across the field by the diggers. The wind sent James their engine noise in gusts, too.

He looked ahead, towards the airport, and saw a blue train

crossing the field immediately beyond the perimeter fence. The railway line would have to join up with the tracks at the end of Montgomery Avenue somehow but James couldn't see how it could be done without a large detour. If they put a pavement next to the tracks you would be able to walk all the way home without crossing a road. The track had been a railway and then it had been a cycle path and now it was a railway again. His mother said, 'The only socialism we're likely to see in Scotland unless we have another referendum.'

He saw a patch of red close by and slid down a high slope towards it. Gathering momentum, barely in control, he just avoided a jagged can lid at his feet. It looked like the blade of a miniature circular saw. His father was out of his line of vision, including lookbacks.

Once safely in the hollow James put the half-filled bag down and searched for the first red tomato. Surrounded by tall heaps of rubbish it was sheltered here and the plants grew luxuriantly.

There were a dozen or so large appliances, cookers, washing machines and even fridges. They were grouped in a rough circle, in groups of twos and threes in the round, as if the hollow had once been a meeting place, as if somehow the people who used to meet were now these big metal boxes. The vegetation grew around, over and through them.

*

There was a huge red beauty of a tomato just by his knee.

He reached down to pick it.

The shock of another voice: 'This is my patch!'

A hooded figure rose up from behind an Electrolux fridge.

He/she was about James's own height. His/her hand held one of the outsize tomatoes, ripe, latent. This grenade was the same kind of tomato James had been about to harvest, a 'beef tomato'. The arm was poised to throw. .

He ungrasped the tomato he had been about to pick. He had the exaggerated gesture of a cowboy, outnumbered or outsmarted, asked to drop his weapon.

He stood up properly, looking towards the covered face of the figure. No, he still couldn't see eyes, nose or lips. He couldn't see if the fridge creature was a boy or a girl. The black hood of a snorkel coat concealed all signs.

He/She was clearly hesitating.

James looked at the huge tomato in his challenger's hand, the arm a primed catapult. The fruit was a deep red, overripe. Maybe, he thought, it was about the size of a heart in a transplant situation.

'Are you a protestant or a catholic?' James called out.

*

It was what Mikey Johnson at school said you should always ask.

James had not used this greeting technique until now.

He didn't really know what a protestant or a catholic was. They did go to different schools, though, and he'd heard that catholics thought his school was a protestant school even though Mikey and Miss Grant said it was for everyone, and the Flemings didn't even go to church.

Mikey Johnson said that Mikey Johnson was a protestant and Mikey Johnson didn't care who knew it.

James didn't mind *not* knowing it.

James's father had said if anyone asked whether you were a 'prod' or a 'tim', you were just to say 'a human being'.

'Are you a protestant or a catholic?' James called out.

*

The beef tomato hit him hard on the side of the head.

It hurt harder than a tomato should. A full slap.

Juice had spurted onto his hair and into his ear.

*

James knew he was crying but he was ducking down, too. He was crying but then he was fumbling in his bag for ammunition.

He grabbed a couple of green tomatoes and threw them awkwardly at his attacker. She/He remained standing where they were. Both tomatoes missed.

Now James was moving on, scuttling across the tomato lands, moving round behind the figure, who had hardly moved.

He wasn't crying now and he hadn't been crying in the first place, OK?

He was behind him/her and closer than before. He threw a tomato and this time he was on target: it thudded into the stupid coat between the shoulder blades.

The figure just stood there like that, a living scarecrow, so James threw three more in succession, harder, faster. They hit the assailant's back in the same place but didn't split as his enemy's had.

'Say something!' he shouted, taking cover behind a

washing machine.

James cleared the tears from his face with the back of his hand and then touched his wounded ear with the tips of his fingers: it was sore, tender and hot. A tomato pip got caught under one of his fingernails as he tried to wipe the juice away.

'What did you hit me for?' he shouted, keeking out at the side. 'This dump is public property! No-one owns the rubbish!'

The figure turned towards him but again James could not see the face properly within the hood.

'I'm a human being!' the voice shouted at him.

The figure raised an arm again, slowly, and shot, fast. James felt another beef tomato whack into him, hitting him on the forehead, hard. It sent tomato juice into his eyes and knocked him off balance. He stumbled and cut his hand trying to break his fall, banging his head against an exposed edge of the machine. It wasn't a bad cut on his hand, but now, yes, his head 'stung'.

He crouched into himself, down low at the machine's side, peering out towards the tomato field, trying to see where his attacker was. No sign, now.

*

He kept watch like that, using the washing machine's open door as a kind of body armour. Gradually he began to relax his guard. Presently he looked around for the object that had hurt his hand and saw an open blade. He dug out a knife. It had the words 'Fort William' on its wood-effect handle.

*

Now he was in the middle of a cloud of thick earthy dust. The wind had changed direction and was sending the disturbed earth from the vast diggers his way. He could see little further than a yard (think of a metre as about a yard said Miss Grant). He narrowed his eyes to stop the grit getting in. He put the knife in the bag and stood up, but he was no longer sure which direction to follow to find his father.

He walked in what he thought would be a straight line, hoping to come to one of the site's edges at least. He could then follow the perimeter fence round to the car park.

The dust blew across in gusts. Visibility veered, sometimes three or four yards (which is round about three or four metres), sometimes zero.

Head down, watching his feet, he walked into the dust.

*

A black and white dog, a collie, crossed into his reduced line of vision. It barked tentatively, wagged its tail, quickly disappeared again.

At one point he heard what must have been the little blue train and he thought again of following the railway line back to Montgomery Avenue. But it was best not to stray from the plan, his father always said that, and he kept on walking straight ahead.

Once he thought he saw the snorkel-coated figure. He/she was at the edges of what could be seen.

He shouted out to his attacker: 'Friends?', but there was a flap and his double turned into an dark piece of matting, an old car carpet caught on an isolated fence pole, a creature wanting to be airborne in the bluster. The carpet had holes for a car's front seats. It flew towards him like a large black seabird until it was brought short by the pole. Then it was unsnagged, borne away from him by the strengthening wind, finally able to free itself.

*

He began to sing the fragments of a song his mother sung 'Hey ebo, ebo, Ebonettes!' and 'The Skip they do's the double dutch, that's them dancing!' This helped him concentrate and it cheered him up a little. You could march to it.

*

He became aware of a growling and screeching, a combined noise, yes, of the diggers and their trail of seagulls. The noise grew louder and louder until James was clambering over the deep muddy tracks the machines had just made with their wheeled chains.

They were too close.

He broke into a run across a high thick wave of sound. The sound was behind him, across him, ahead of him.

He tripped but got up quickly and managed to reach the mesh of the perimeter fence. He turned around, pressing his back to the wire. One of the vast yellow diggers passed just in front of him, seagulls above in glimpses of calls and cries of white. He shouted to the driver high up in the cab, but no-one heard or saw him.

*

He bent down on his haunches, holding onto the harsh chain-link with the fingers of one hand. They were the fronds of a sweet-pea against an industrial fence. His other hand was a trembling fist.

He made himself shiver and then closed his eyes tight.

*

'How much you got there, Jim?'

His father's voice was soft, too soft for him to be truly matter-of-fact. He put his hand on James's shoulder and the boy uncurled from his hunkered-down freeze.

He stood up, glancing at his father's face without looking into his eyes.

He untied the bag and offered up the miserable few green tomatoes. He wouldn't be about to cry if his dad wasn't being so stupidly gentle.

'Hey, that's not bad for a beginner. And you've found a piece of history, too.' He took the knife from the bag. There was just a catch to his dad's voice.

'Fort William, eh? We should all drive up there sometime, have a look at the Highlands. Maybe not stop for long, can be on the wet side...'

James said something or he didn't say something or some sort of sound anyway.

'Come on,' his father said, 'better get these back to the car. It'll be a bumper year for tomato chutney, eh?.'

The diggers had stopped work, the new silence was solid. James could see the car a hundred yards away, the last in the car park. They began to make their way across the dump, James at first with a stagger. He had pins and needles from crouching so long.

'Don't tell Mum –' his father said and James looked up – he had been just about to say that. He met his father's look – 'but I've never been that keen on chutney.'

'Me neither.' James said.

His father slung all the bags on one shoulder and picked James up in his arms. 'I don't think Mum likes it, either,' his father said, adjusting the balance of the bags, lengthening his stride.

The Call

Tim Sykes

O NE A.M.
  'Man born shelterless,' he said. 'Nature hostile.' He gestured to T with the baby in the sling. 'Father gives up all strength to child. Child prospers, father weakens, dies.'

With the beard and the accent he looked like a Russian writer or something, if you set aside the fact he was a mad wino outside a 24-hour Tesco Metro.

'...Father uses up strength – protects child from frost, hunger, wild beast. You spare some change?'

Nikolai or Fyodor had a point.

T entered the shop. The baby stuff was at the far end. Seemed they didn't stock any gripe water. But the baby had fallen asleep already, to the beat of his heart. T roamed the aisles. Unending rows of pasta sauce. Fluorescent dreamworld. The baby pursed his lips. His miniature face twisted in grief, though his eyes stayed shut.

T made for the exit. London's twenty-sixth safest borough, it soothed the night terrors.

'Tell you this for free,' said the Russian through his beard, '– common task of mankind is sons stop procreation, instead figure out how we resurrect fathers who expended life-force...'

The pavement was greasy orange. T stroked his baby's furry head.

Some clubbers were shrieking but they looked confused when they noticed the sling and the baby.

T passed the police sign further down the high street:

CAN YOU HELP US? SERIOUS ASSAULT.

A fox came trotting down the road, sniffing at the recycling bins. Thursday tomorrow. The fox kind of acknowledged T as it passed. It was the dad from the family that lived behind the railway.

T turned into the street his home was on.

He kissed the baby's nose.

A hoarse, shrill voice, almost human, barked out somewhere in the night.

*

Something hissed.

Where was the baby? Had he smothered it? T rolled over.

'Eating mouse is immoral,' said the big sister.

T sat up. Where did the baby go? He squinted. Marky Mark was dangling by his front paws, wearing a foul expression, from the clutches of Big Sis. It was past six-thirty.

'I put scraps out.'

'Well done love,' said T.

'Mum's having breakfast.'

T sat on the windowsill with Big Sis and Marky Mark the cat. The scraps hadn't been touched. The bowl rested in the long grass near the space hopper. Behind them the bank rose steeply to the railway tracks. Should try and pop in on Dad today, poor thing, or tomorrow. T breathed on the window and wiped the fog away. A couple of weeks ago both the fox parents had appeared in the garden together with three cubs. Really sweet they were. But lately they'd only seen the dog fox. Always rushed and harassed. No one knew where the vixen had gone.

C loomed in the doorframe.

'Fed the baby, did the nappy change and made food for us all,' she said, kissing T, 'so you could sleep in and look for wildlife.'

'Dude and I were up half the night with the ol' colic. Had to take the new kid round the block.'

'I heard you – slammed the front door at half one.'

'Seemed like you slept through it.'

They cuddled.

T patted C on the back to tell her he needed to wash and go to work.

*

It wouldn't have hurt to let Big Sis wait up a few more minutes. End up choosing between looking in on your own dad and getting to say nighty night. T nuzzled Big Sis's ear. He whispered about monkeys and banana skins, so the little girl would have funny dreams.

T got out his phone. Eight o'clock. C was still settling the baby downstairs. Dad had sat there, smiling the whole time, in an armchair facing the wall. 'Oh, really?' he kept saying, 'Oh, really?'

The baby quietened. T tiptoed down the stairs. He dropped

onto the sofa next to C.

The cat went out the dog-flap. The draught brought a whiff of fox into the lounge.

'Need to board that thing up,' said C.

'What's Marky going to do?'

T rested his head on C's lap.

'Not the cat I'm concerned about. Size-S perverts crawling into our living room's what I'm concerned about.'

'Doubt any paedo could handle the crying. Anyway, if it's just a small one I can probably take him.'

'The fully grown paedos don't need to break in. Just wait till the early hours for you to bring baby out to them.'

T yawned and sat up.

'No one's going to mug a man with a baby. I never felt safer.'

'You used our son as a human shield?'

'Kind of. Got him to sleep though.'

C giggled.

The carry-cot coughed. They froze. Coughing stopped.

'So how was your day?' said T. 'Thursdays is what, infant yoga, jazz babies? Dad wasn't good by the way.'

C switched on the telly with the sound muted and went through the channels. Might as well stick with the wildlife one when you can't hear what they're saying. There are worse places than Alaska. Marky Mark sprang back in through the dog-flap, noticed T, padded over to him with his stripy tail up. The smell from the garden followed him into the room.

'Your fox is rank,' said C. 'Some close friend ought to have a little word with him.'

'Stressful being a single dad. You don't get what it's like.'

'Being a single dad?'

'…family to feed.'

'They don't cramp his style. He still gets out and about. I gather that's important.' C traced a spiral on the back of T's hand.

T got up.

'Need anything from the shop?' he said.

'Can't be doing with foxes smearing germs where Big Sis plays,' said C, '– however relatable you find them.'

Marky Mark followed T down the street as far as the corner. On the main road it was cold and quiet, like Alaska. A bit of drizzle. The Russian or Pole was outside Tescos again with his purple skin and manky whiskers. He rose to meet T.

'You not bring child tonight,' he said. 'Children use up my life-force then leaving me afterwards on street. Children don't want to know father no more.' He raised his can of own-brand. 'Children is sacred blessing.'

T walked on. Poor Dad. Almost seemed like he recognised T this afternoon. 'Oh, really?' he'd said.

T took off his coat to feel unsheltered.

His phone rang. C.

'It got in the house. Went for Arthur…'

He pelted.

The fox was still ambling along, sort of smirking, when T rounded the corner. It took off at the sight of him. Guilty conscience. He'd catch it though. It disappeared under a van.

C was crying at the front door, squeezing the baby.

'It was about to take him, T, like a hen.'

The baby was fast asleep.

'I'm blocking it,' said T. 'Right away.'

He let go of C and sat on the floor to look at the dog-flap.

Nail a bit of wood across for now. Block it up properly later, try to fit a cat one, with a magnet. Meantime he was going to get the fox. Do the necessary. The little ones too. Maybe he'd be bitten in the process. Be infected, hospitalised…

A sound came from upstairs. T started. A train clattered past the gardens. T listened. The sound came again from the bedroom. It was spasmodic and harsh. Big Sis was laughing in her sleep.

The Jim Hangovers

Rodge Glass

LIKE ALL MY FRIENDS, I SEE HIM LESS OFTEN NOW I'M A DAD. That's what I say on the rare occasions when people ask how Jim is doing these days, thinking I'll know. But somehow it's been eight years. Nearly eight and a half. It's not just that I don't know how to explain the passage of all that time - the idea is so upside down, so inside out, that despite the evidence I wonder if it's a trick. And if that's the case, I think, then who's tricking me? Already, you can see. How the mind works. In the dark. Doing the washing up. Cleaning the high chair. Whatever. Now sit still for a second while I put this thing round your neck.

At the time it didn't feel temporary. But perhaps it wasn't that long at all, just a sliver of time between one me and another, neither of which were really me at all. For three or four years during my twenties I'd be out several nights a week with Jim, at parties, at clubs, at gigs. Or more often, let's be honest shall we, just in some side street pub where the toilet floors were wet and you tried not to think about why as the dampness seeped through to your socks. If no one else was free, or game, then it was just the two of us, taking our future successes for granted, toasting anything we could think of, despite the fact that we were the kind of punters who drank on a Monday afternoon, on a Sunday morning, whenever the shutters were open and we weren't on shift.

We had minimum wage jobs of course, like everyone else we knew, like you will too. Forty-five, fifty hours a week. Pub jobs. Call centre jobs. Night shifts. Cold calling. If we were cast into the employment wilderness for hangover offences then hey, there was always another just an application form and a fake reference away. I suppose these were 'boom times', but that term was coined by, as Jim liked to say, men living on the moon, men who actually notice the difference between economic highs and lows. Back then, those guys drank in different places to us. Who knows where they are now, probably still knocking them back on the moon. And meanwhile here I am, with you, at dawn, nearly eight and a half years dry. Sometimes we'll be doing this early shift together, I'll pick a chunk of porridge or apple out of your hair and think: the thousands of photos we have, they're somehow not enough. Whole days have gone undocumented. Whole hours of your evolution have been lost. Then I remember that for years I had no camera. Once a pint is finished, it's dead, that's what they call it. And after a drink dies, all you do is order a fresh and try not to think too much. There's no need to record the bloody thing for posterity.

Now I think about it – I mean, now I've actually got to focus for a second and remember my own life – I've no idea where our money for the next round came from. It seemed like everything was free in those days – or maybe it was just that, apart from the drinks, there was nothing else to pay for. It's not like we sent birthday cards to our sisters. Yes, Christmas was marked, toasted, licked and sucked dry, but each year we balked at the price of a train ticket home. Jim was

a fundamentalist. He thought he was Orwell or something –
poor Jim, Down and Out in wherever the fuck, nobly doing
the dishes in some backstreet Vietnamese restaurant, being
watched over by his future biographers. He thought he was
Bolaño, the lank-haired, struggling poet, and London was
Mexico City in the 70s. I didn't know this at the time – I didn't
read Bolaño during those years, I didn't read anyone, I wasn't
awake yet – but Bolaño said his entire output was a love letter
to his 'lost generation'. By which he meant: the Chileans, the
Uruguayans, the Argentines, whose countries were ransacked
by dictatorships which drove them to new homes they didn't
seek across the world – in short, a generation with proper
fucking problems. When I first heard that thing about the love
letter it was out of Jim's mouth and all I thought was, what a
thing to pour all your energy into: the past. But now I can see.

If I could remember it, I'd detail mine too. Right down
to the slurred end-of-night babble, the early-morning Jim
hugs, the Jim promises. You might be interested when you're
older. Okay, it's no dictatorship, it's not worth a dedication
but I'm sorry, if I trip in the street and I'm heading for the
pavement, head first, arms not quite fast enough to thrust
outwards, it's probably what I'll be thinking about. Still trying
to work it all out. Why wouldn't you occur to me? Well, you
live in a different part of the mind. One without stains. Thank
God, your mother's still there too – there's a lot to say thank
you for, right? My own father, your Granddaddy – not my
mother's biggest fan. Not Chairman of the Fan Club. Not even
a fucking member. Whereas, this old romantic? I watch you
yawn just the way she does, like a tiger waking up, pawing the
air and I think: fuck Jim. We're fine. Still, there's nothing you
can do. It's the Jims of this world that pick away at you in the

night, multiplying, recycling themselves. Whispering: are you sure you got that right? Now, have some of this please. That's good. Isn't that tasty?

We were always looking for excuses. The birthday of some distant friend would do fine. Someone's brother coming to town. Anything. At first that was enough, but soon there weren't enough birthdays, enough brothers, enough New Year's Eves or Bank Holiday weekends to keep us afloat. And it seemed like everyone else we knew just wasn't as thirsty. So after that, if there was no occasion, and Jim and I wanted a night out, we'd *research* one. And in the days before internet phones, you needed an imagination for that. So we looked up our occasions in the diary Jim used to get posted from his Mum every year, then leave blank, as a way to spite her – *Ha! Take that mother! I'm not going to do ANYTHING with my life!* She was a real woman, Jim's mum. She kept posting those things every year. She kept calling. Which I think about more than you might expect. I find myself staring at my computer asking myself: will you let the phone ring out when I call? How long before you work me out? And: will I send you diaries? Now, that's dangerous thinking. If a man allows himself to think like that, he's half way to letting go of the balloon, do you know what I mean? But then, by the time you're thinking about stopping yourself thinking, it's already much too late. So I give in to it, and daydream. I think, what will we do when you're grown, me and your mother? Maybe we'll be fine. Maybe we'll be one of those couples who buys a boat and sails round the world on extended second honeymoon, meeting other retirees, making love like teenagers, mourning our lost parenting years – *What were we thinking of? And really, what did we expect?* Or maybe I'll wake up one day with a hangover, your mother a hologram, a mirage, a memory, and I'll be back in the pub with Jim and his fucking diary. It's that kind of thinking that stops me picking up the phone.

It didn't just tell you about Easter, American Independence Day, Australia Day, yadda yadda, but was littered with information in italicized letters under each date. In Bar Italia in Soho, we celebrated the anniversary of the day Mussolini founded the Italian Fascist Party (February 23rd, 1919) with three bottles of their finest vino. In the High Baller near Charing Cross, it was the anniversary of when Ellen Church became the first airline stewardess (May 15th, 1930), and we drank Mojitos and Margaritas until they kicked us out around four. It went on. Shakespeare's marriage to Anne Hathaway (November 27th, 1582) celebrated – where else? – the bar at the Globe theatre. The publication of *Alice in Wonderland* (2nd August, 1865) celebrated I can't remember where. Really, we wrung it out. A rumour started up that this was all part of some pretentious art project. That it was going to lead to something. A girlfriend of Jim's said we were misunderstood geniuses. Which says something about the crowd we hung out with. It never occurred to anyone that we were just losing, and didn't know how to turn the game around.

There were pits I lived in during that period that I hardly spent time in, except to collapse on the bed sometime after midnight, the memories of my late-night talks with Jim already slipping out of my mind as I lay on the half-broken mattress, stretched out, only half-aware of what was happening. Our conversations, mostly vague plans, slipped into the air, the details hazy. Then they became distant, then they were gone. One morning, shovelling dry cereal into my mouth, I believed the conversation Jim and I had the night before had morphed somehow into a cousin, a distant one whose name I couldn't quite remember at the family wedding. There was an exchange with this cousin, and me, and my own father, by the dance floor. Dad said, *What's wrong, don't you know your own people?* Of course that's impossible, how can a conversation turn into a human being? How can an orange also be a brick? These are the things I thought about. Usually, the Jim hangovers lasted a few days. Or until the next night out. That was the best way of getting rid of them. Some days, even now, in this stark dawn light, in our garden, when I'm holding you tight, if I close my eyes and concentrate I can still feel the bile at the back of my throat. And I can't believe I got away with it.

The day C.S. Lewis was born (29th November, 1898), we had a fight outside The Rock off Leicester Square. About what? How could I tell you? Anyway, a few days later, on the street, Jim and I embraced like brothers. We kissed each other on both cheeks. We had to be reminded of how we'd howled, denouncing each other. When a friend explained our bruises, we laughed like it was the funniest joke we'd ever heard, then toasted our eternal friendship. That's how those times were, don't look at me like that. We tricked ourselves into thinking we were immortal. As Jim once said, in the Poet's Palace I think, raising twin drams of whisky and toasting the death of Robert Burns in Dumfries (July 21st, 1796): *How do I even know you exist, man? How do I know I'm not the only thing that's real in this world, and you're just a figment of my imagination?* No danger of that sort of talk these days. Though at the time, it seemed likely. Maybe I was nothing. Not anywhere, except in Jim's mind.

I know, I know. Open wide.

This continued, on and off, for too long. Jim would phone

after his shift finished, sometimes I was still on shift myself: *Hey, you do know it's the anniversary of the day China launched its first satellite, right? The day a patent was finally granted for the thimble? The day the first Hawaiian stamps were issued?* And off we'd go, nothing to do except waste our youth. Which was, as Jim always used to say, our sacred right. We had been born lucky. In the right century, the right continent, the right city, the right *gender*. (Congratulations, son. That's you too.) Our lives, Jim reminded me, while trying to get the barmaid's attention, were easier than most of the major boozers in history could ever have imagined. We might not be rich, well connected, have any obvious talents or great intellect, but at least there was no black death for us, no conscription, no Wall Street Crash. We always had company, conversation, and enough for the next drink. Meanwhile there was plenty of time to turn the game around, and the nighttime did a pretty good job of blocking out the day.

Another spoonful. That's it. Good boy.

The more we drank, the more people we seemed to meet on our travels round the city. We recognized kindred spirits in the pubs and the style bars and the dives and the cooler-than-thou hotspots which are probably all renovated as something else now. And that's fine. Not everything needs to last to be worth something. The band doesn't have to stick together until everyone dies, the songs can't be unwritten. If they were great songs once, they'll be great songs forever, regardless of anyone's playing them. Which sounds like something Jim would say, but it's one of mine. Me, doing a Jim impression. Of The Jim that Used to Be. Maybe he's a dad now too, sitting in some patterned living room, three-year-old girl on his knee, gently brushing her hair while she watches TV, thinking: I can't believe I got away with it. I doubt it. But then, maybe he doubted me too.

Though we hardly ever knew their names, it felt like we were making friends in those places we used to go. Some serious drinkers, some just letting loose for the night. Some regulars from the city, some just passing through. We crossed people doing the same things, circling each other, recognizing some faces from past nights out, house parties; as the nights went on, we noticed friends of friends, lovers, ex-girlfriends of ex-girlfriends, the whole rainbow. During the parties, it seemed like all of London was full of people who had no reason to get up in the morning. Nothing better to do than tell stories to each other of past exploits, leaving out certain parts of course. Chopping off the start of the tale. The real ending. Cutting out characters. *Reshaping truth for the target audience*, as Jim put it, with that shit-eating grin. Come on now, a little more. Nearly finished.

You're probably wondering who I am now, but a few times on these tours of the city we even ended up sleeping on the floors of complete strangers, at the end of parties, feeling totally safe, because we thought these people were like us. And, Jim would say, wasn't that special? Didn't that make you feel you were part of something – even if that something was just the mass of idiots trying to forget? *Forget what?* I asked. *Why do you always have to bring it back to that?* Sometimes, I swear to God, I had no idea what he was talking about. At the swings yesterday, while I was watching you fly back and forth, back and forth, your face alight, I thought about looking Jim up. These days, it's easier, right? I could probably find him in a day or two. Maybe, I thought, we could just go for one drink. We could talk about our kids, how surprised we were to find ourselves at ease in our own skins after all. You knew what I was thinking, or it seemed like you did. You held your arms up, wanted out of the swing, started crying - so I plucked you up out of the swing and carried you home, kissing those cheeks. Thinking: no. Thinking: maybe I should look up everyone I knew in those days, everyone *apart* from Jim, and tell them I'm sorry.

There were occasional relationships in amongst all these, but these always seemed to run out of energy after a few weeks or less and send us springing back to each other, and to the bars. We were still pretending, something I only realized after the Swiss girl from the punk collective I'd been in love with for two weeks (Heidi? Helga? Helen?) picked her clothes up off the floor, dressed herself and explained, calm as yoga, that she'd better get home to make her boyfriend breakfast now. *Mm*, I answered, not knowing how to. *Better get those eggs on*. What I meant was, this has to stop. I phoned Jim but didn't even have the chance to get started. *Don't tell me*, he said, cutting in. *Michelangelo's David. Unveiled in Florence, this day in 1504. Don't panic, comrade – if we're quick, we can be catatonic by mid-afternoon.* A few days later was 9/11, and we went out as usual. If the world was coming to an end, said Jim, then why not? What else could we do but welcome oblivion? Besides, it was 9/11 somewhere every day. Bolaño's was in 1973.

The pubs weren't exactly empty that night, but they weren't full either. Jim was telling me what it all meant, the way he saw things, what was coming for us all. But he wasn't really talking to me. I got up from the booth and said I was going to the toilet. That I'd be back in a minute. But the door to the toilet was near the exit. I took a left instead of a right.

I wonder how long he sat there for.

In the Marshes

Iain Robinson

HAMISH WATCHED HIS DAUGHTERS PLAYING CHASE through the long grass, arching their backs to avoid each other's touch, their squeals cutting through the cooling air. Beyond them he could see the thicket of blackthorn, hornbeam, and elder, where he'd lose his football, emerging from it later with his arms scraped and bloodied from the search. This common was where he'd hung out with Chris and Ade that long summer before uni. Now his daughters were playing on it. Unimaginable, twenty-three years ago. On this turf he was both eighteen and forty-one, his friend Chris was both alive and already two decades gone, his daughters were both inconceivable and startling in their presence. 'Are we going home?'

It was Maggie, his eldest, her cheeks flushed from the chase and the cold air. Mary stumbled up beside her.

He smiled at them. They were beautiful. His joy tangled in loss.

'It's getting a little late,' he said, turning towards the lane. 'Time for tea.'

'Not now,' said Mary, dragging the words out into a whine. 'We have to play more.'

Mary never wanted to eat, life was too urgent. He

prepared himself for a tussle of wills, but found that Maggie was hopping from one foot to another, her mouth puckered up in that way she had when she was thinking.

'We can feed the birds, before tea. Can we? Can we, Dad?'

Mary jumped up and down, Maggie's shadow, her echo. 'Can we? Can we?'

He nodded and they followed the lane, the girls running ahead, their wellies a little loose, long shadows dancing ahead of them. It was something Annie would have commented on, shared with him. He didn't want to meet anyone, not just yet. He wanted, he wasn't sure what, to heal perhaps, to have space. Perhaps that was why he'd come back, after so much time, because in London, where he'd spent the bulk of those twenty-three years, the memories were far denser, more unbearable, echoes of his former selves, and of Annie, layering and amplifying in the air in every familiar haunt.

The girls turned up the drive and when he got them back in sight they were crowding around Ade, who was waiting by the cottage, leaning against his little red van. They lived in the end cottage, an extended former estate worker's home with flinty walls and grey roof slates. Its three small bedrooms and little walled garden felt like luxuries after their Battersea flat. There was money left over from the sale, enough to see them through the year until he'd worked out his next steps.

Ade stubbed out his ciggie and crouched down, letting the girls hug him before they raced off through the gate into the garden.

'I was passing by,' he said, as Hamish approached. 'Bad timing?'

Ade had his back to the sun, and Hamish had to shade his eyes to read his mood.

'Just about to sling something in the oven for the girls. Beer?'

Ade was still in his overalls. His boots were flecked all over with paint.

'Won't stay long,' he replied, with a nod.

Hamish unlocked the front door and went through to the kitchen, where he could keep an eye on the girls in the garden. Maggie had taken her bag of bread crusts and cheese crumbs from her pocket and was standing on the wooden bench, shielding her eyes to scan the sky. Mary was clambering up beside her, eager for the show. Hamish took two tins from the fridge, opened them, handed one to Ade.

'Watch,' he said.

Maggie was on tiptoes, her arms outstretched. From her fists she let the crumbled food fall. A shadow dropped from the sun, then another, and within a few seconds there were six or seven jackdaws on the patio, strutting around the bench, taking the food in their beaks and angling their heads to watch Maggie's fingers with their pale grey eyes. Mary clung to the arm of the bench, a little afraid. Maggie let more food fall. Another group of birds came down, a pair of magpies getting in on the action, a jay, more jackdaws.

'That isn't right,' said Ade.

'It's fine. I think they like her.'

'They're vermin.'

'They're clever.'

Hamish considered telling Ade about the gifts, but thought he wouldn't understand that, wouldn't want to hear it.

'Vermin. Scavengers. You're just cold meat to them, a future meal.'

'Maybe.' Hamish turned to face his old friend. 'Look,

what's up? You're here for a reason. I can tell.'

'It's nearly twenty-four years, this weekend, that's all.'

'Chris?'

Ade nodded. 'We haven't talked about him much, since you came back.'

'It's a long time ago.'

'Not for me it isn't.'

'Look, I've had other things to deal with, you know that.'

'I just think, we ought to talk, properly like, about what happened that night.'

Hamish shook his head. He'd been over it all in his mind so many times before. The last hours before Chris went missing. The police had questioned him a couple of times. For a while he thought they suspected him. They'd searched the marshes, in dinghies and with divers, but nothing had been found. After seven years Chris was declared legally dead. But that was all two decades ago, and it didn't seem important coming back here. In the months since Annie's death he hadn't even considered it, that anyone would remember, but then there was Ade.

Hamish sighed. 'I don't want to drag it all up again, not now, especially not now.'

'He's out there somewhere.' Ade flushed, pacing to the door and back again. 'Don't you want to find him?'

'Come on, Ade.'

'I see.' He placed the beer tin on the worktop. 'I got to go anyway.'

'It's not that,' Hamish called after him. He heard the door of the van slam and the engine start.

He sighed again and tipped the dregs of Ade's beer fizzing into the sink. Outside Maggie had run out of food to throw.

The birds suddenly peeled away in ones and twos until the garden was bare and silent. Maggie jumped down from the bench and Mary followed her. The crumbs were gone, but Maggie found a stick and poked about among the paving stones and the long grass of the lawn. After a while she bent down and came back up with something in her hand. Her reward. They both came running, panting, through the kitchen door.

'Did you see? Did you see?'

'I saw.'

She held it up for him. It was an old bolt this time, a little rusty.

'Wash it and put it with the others.'

Maggie nodded but her eyes were searching the room behind him. 'Where's Ade?'

Hamish tousled her hair. 'He had to go. Come on, supper will be ready soon.'

*

It was dark by the time Hamish got the girls settled in their beds. They shared a bedroom, which left him the smallest room to use as a study. He switched on the laptop, let it boot up. He did a little freelance content writing to tide things over, but it wouldn't be enough in the long term, when the money from the flat sale ran out. Besides, he didn't think he had it in him to continue as things were. He needed to start over.

In their old flat he would lay the table for four, without thinking, sometimes even dish out a fourth plate. Maggie would be the one who'd notice first, tell him it was ok, and help him take things back to the kitchen. It wasn't fair on her, of course. He tried only to cry when he was alone, at night, when he thought they were asleep, but one day Maggie told him she could hear him, that it kept her awake. Moving here was what made most sense, to get the girls playing on the common, walking along the marshes, all under the big open skies. It was a place where you could grow unfettered. He couldn't bring Annie back, but he could give them the air and the land.

He tried to write for a while, and then retreated downstairs. He enjoyed the quiet once the girls were asleep. After the constant rumble of the city, the silence and the darkness felt odd, both familiar and disconcerting. He knew he should call Ade. Now would be the time to talk. He hadn't seen Ade for ten years before a couple of months ago and their reunions had centred on getting their kids together. He had a girl a year older than Maggie, and two boys, the youngest of which would be in Mary's class when she started in reception after the summer. He'd gleaned enough to know that Ade hadn't moved on much from what had happened. Perhaps because he had stayed here it felt more urgent to him. Ade said he dreamed about Chris, felt his presence. Hamish put this down to the influence of Lucy, Ade's wife. She was full of pseudo-science and superstition, crystals and amulets.

He remembered Maggie's gift and pulled out the organiser box he'd bought for her at the hardware store. It was meant for grading screws and nails, but the little compartments were ideal for sorting out the odd array of detritus the birds delivered to her. It was her treasure chest. One tray contained pieces of plastic, mainly beads and broken toys, sorted by size and colour. Another tray had metal things, screws, nails, bottle tops and so on. He was a little alarmed at first.

Maggie had started feeding them by accident, dropping bits of sandwiches while waiting for the school bus. Within a week, the jackdaws were gathering for her, swooping down when they saw her leave the cottage and strutting about in her wake. It took about a month before the gifts started to appear. It was as if they were paying her back, that they knew these objects belonged in Maggie's world, were what they could feed her in return. Hamish didn't mind encouraging it. Maggie was smiling again. Her bedwetting had stopped.

The top tray was full of pottery fragments, as if from an archaeological dig. A number of them had letters, probably from one of those plates with writing along its borders. They reminded Hamish of scrabble tiles. He pulled them out of their compartments and slid them around the coffee table until he had them in a line.

'What are you doing?'

He jolted. He hadn't heard Mary on the stairs. Her step was so light. She ran over to him in her nightie, her bunny, Casper, hugged tightly to her chest.

'That's Maggie's treasure,' she said, clambering onto his lap.

He stroked her hair. 'Couldn't you sleep?'

She lowered her eyes and shook her head.

'What's up?'

'Are we all going to die?'

He hesitated, wondering how to answer. 'Not for a very long time.'

'All of us?'

'Yes, but not until we're very old.'

'Was Mummy very old?'

'No.'

Mary didn't speak right way, as if deciding something.

'I don't want to die. I'd miss Casper too much.'

'It won't happen for a long time.'

'Maybe I could die with Casper.'

'Maybe.'

'I think that when all the days have ended, and there are no more days, and there is night forever is when we die.'

He kissed her on the forehead and gradually she slipped back into sleep. Then he carried her back to her bed and returned to the living room. He felt like crying, but somehow it wouldn't come, and instead he slumped in the armchair, suddenly exhausted. Annie was told the cancer was inoperable, that she had weeks left, as soon as it was diagnosed. She died two months later. If she'd had longer there would have been time to prepare, for things to be dignified, for her to be ready. But she didn't have longer and she wasn't ready. All her bravery couldn't mask the fear, her blind cold panic at the swiftness of it all. It wasn't fair, that she had life robbed away, and Chris had thrown his up so willingly. That night they'd been on the common smoking pot, listening to Nirvana on Ade's tape deck. Ade had gone home to sneak a few beers out from his Dad's crate. Chris was restless, agitated. He had his scramble bike with him. He'd split with Emma, and although it had happened before, Hamish thought this time it was final. In September Emma would be going to uni. Chris wouldn't. His future was all mapped out for him in his Dad's garage. No choice in the matter. He was being left behind. Ade was off to college to study horticulture, not that anything came of it. Hamish was heading to London. They talked about Emma and the next year and of how Hamish would introduce him to the girls he'd meet at uni. It had all felt like a lie, somehow. He remembered Chris standing and pulling on his helmet. 'Going for a ride,' he said. 'The marshes in this moonlight will be something else.' Then he mounted the bike, kicked the engine into life, and was gone.

Hamish realised he was drifting. He leaned forward, the fragments of broken plate were where he'd left them on the table. He slid them gently about the tabletop with his fingertips, seeking out words. He was hoping for something, he realised. A message. From who? How? He dismissed the idea. It was late and he was tired. The girls would wake him early. He scooped up the fragments into his palms, returned them to their places in the box. They reminded him less of scrabble tiles now and more of runes or a Ouija board. Any words would have been formed by pure chance, whatever they said would carry no intention. It was just the sort of nonsense Lucy would love. He was glad that Ade hadn't seen him at it.

*

Saturday came cool and bright. They were walking the path that ran the length of one of the ditches that drained the fields on either side. Fields green with sugar beet. Up ahead he could see the wood. The jackdaws had their colonies in the beech trees alongside the larger rookeries. The beech trees gave way to alder and willow as the ground became wetter. Beyond this lay the marshes.

Maggie and Mary walked a little way ahead, their backpacks overfilled with soft toys. Every so often a jackdaw or magpie would swoop and settle in the field, nearby, scuffing the flinty soil for worms with claws and beaks, or strutting alongside them for a while before taking flight. Maggie had her own escort. It was a path he knew well, from childhood walks with his parents to later adventures with Chris and Ade, the route they'd take to their den in the wood with its illicit hoard of cider and pot.

The sound of the roads fell away. Hamish could hear the girls' songs and chants, their little incantations to the moment, the crunch of their feet on the track, the hoarse cries of the rooks and jackdaws, his own breathing. There was nobody on the path behind them, but even so he kept on feeling the urge to check, as if somebody not far behind was matching their pace.

The harsh calls of the birds grew louder, more incessant, as they circled and squabbled around their nesting places. The path veered away from the dyke to curve through the woods and down to the marshland walk. The wind was rising as the day warmed up. All around was the creaking and shifting of living wood. The ground was becoming boggy, more difficult to tread. The undergrowth of fern and holly brushed and snagged their jeans.

'What's that smell?' asked Mary.

'The bog, silly,' replied Maggie.

'Like poo.'

'Like a toilet.'

It was a peaty smell, of brackish waters and vegetal decay. Hamish enjoyed it.

'Come on, girls. Not much further. We might see some mayflies down by the water.'

He had learned that it was better to get the girls out of the house at the weekends. That way they squabbled less. Even in the cottage, where Annie had never lived, the space she left was tangible, the gap in the sofa, the empty, untouched side of the bed. It was normal to be angry; he didn't need an NHS pamphlet to tell him that. It took him a while to realise that it applied to him as well as the girls. He was angry with Annie, for leaving him alone with the girls, to do singly what they'd started as a team, and have to cope with their loss alongside his own. He needed the fresh air and open skies. In the city he would have become irritable, impatient with the girls. Ade was angry too, still after all this time, and like the girls his anger was displaced and disjointed.

As they broke through into the alder and willow they joined the wetland trail. It was designed to be taken from the car park, its paths and walkways following a sequence of jetties and hides for viewing wildlife. The walkway was raised up from the boggy ground by an inch or two on wooden boards and covered with mesh to stop it getting slippery. The boards had a little give in them, and the girls were jumping, enjoying the effect. The trees and scrub gave way to the water's edge. Across the marshes Hamish could just make out the car park by the glint of a windscreen. It was where they'd found Chris's scramble bike, long before there even was a wetland trail. Hamish never went that way.

All around them there was a shifting and undulating sea of movement as the wind sighed and whinnied through sedge and spike-rush, sweet-grass and whorl-grass, everything a shade of sunlit green and brown. They came to one of the viewing jetties. The girls ran to the edge, and Hamish settled a firm hand on Mary's shoulder.

'Careful, the water's deeper than it looks.'

'It's very peaceful.' Maggie stared thoughtfully over the water. The seed from the hogweed were being caught by the wind, their cotton sails dancing just above head height.

'Fairies,' squealed Mary.

'Not,' shouted Maggie.

Hamish put his hand on her back to calm her. 'What does it make you think of, Mags?'

'Mummy.'

Hamish looked into the water. It was twitching, shifting with life, all manner of skaters and newts, flies and larvae.

'A long time ago people would come here to remember people they'd lost.'

Maggie looked up at him. 'Really? What would they do?'

'Throw their most precious things into the water, swords and rings and so on.'

'That's silly,' said Mary. 'They might need a sword.'

Hamish wasn't really sure if he was right. Did they make their offerings to honour the dead, or to placate them? Perhaps it amounted to the same thing, a way of placating memory, preventing it from harming the mind.

'I think it's lovely,' said Maggie.

The cloud was building and the waters suddenly became darker. Hamish felt restless, uneasy. Ade was right. Chris was probably out here somewhere, in the marshes. What if he was right here, looking up at them? The sun broke through, and Hamish started at the sudden appearance of their reflections, jerking and shaking on the surface of the water.

'Let's go. It's too windy for mayflies.'

The girls followed him reluctantly. They tracked back into the wood and started up the incline to the field.

'Do you think they give anything back?' asked Maggie.

Hamish was puzzled. 'Who?'

'The dead,' she exclaimed. 'All those rings and swords and stuff, thrown into the water. I don't know, it just seems they might give some of it back.'

*

Maggie was up to her knees in birds, wading through them on the lawn. Mary stood on the bench, squealing, but Maggie looked calm, almost unaware of anything but the birds. Her lips moved softly.

'What's she saying to them?' asked Ade.

Hamish shrugged. 'Never can hear.'

They were standing by the back door. Ade had called by after packing up for the day.

'You asked her?'

'It's between her and them.'

Ade flicked the ash from his ciggie into the cold tea dregs at the bottom of his mug and frowned.

'What?' demanded Hamish. 'She's not a witch you know.' He was thinking about the gifts and her treasure chest, how easily it could be misconstrued.

Ade looked at him sharply. 'That's Lucy's area, not mine.' Then he gazed up at the crowns of the beech trees at the end of the lane, and, it seemed to Hamish, beyond, to the marshes and the great blue sky with its whorls of thin white cloud. 'Look, about the other day.'

Hamish cut him off. 'No, I'm sorry about that.'

'What made you think I was going to apologise?' he asked, then he looked down at his feet. 'I know it isn't easy for you. I know that. And I know he's been gone a long time and he won't be found. It's just, well, his Dad died a couple of years ago, not sure if you knew that, but with him gone there's no one but us who really cares that Chris lived at all, no one else who remembers.'

Hamish sighed and looked over at Maggie and Mary. Maggie would remember Annie with some clarity, but he knew that for Mary she was already an abstract, a dream-presence, a visceral yearning tangled with memories of the old flat and of London, and that no matter how many times he flicked through photo albums with her, this was inevitable.

'We'll do something then, to remember him,' said Hamish. 'You and me, perhaps the kids as well, make a day of it in the marshes.'

*

The eastern horizon was greying out. Somewhere, high up, a jet rumbled. Mary ran off ahead to peer into rabbit holes but Maggie hung back, keeping herself a few steps behind Hamish, muttering to herself. He often took them for a walk on the common before bedtime. Hamish thought it tired them out. He enjoyed listening for the evening birds, the thrushes and dunnocks, but that evening the wind carried the incessant cawing of the rookeries, the dry calling of the birds reaching over the long fields. He felt a little better after Ade had gone, that something had been decided on. Mary was howling with delight, her hair coppery in the last of the sunlight, every strand of it picked out. He felt the past being overwritten with new memories.

The damp, black smell of the marshes came with the sound of the birds. The insects hadn't settled yet, and they were being shrouded by midges. Maggie was still mumbling, and Hamish wondered, for a moment, if a friend had joined her, one of the kids from her class or Ade's daughter. He turned to look back at her, but she was alone. She scuffed through the grass, her eyes down. She had a small object in her hand that she was toying with, rubbing between her thumb and forefinger like a worry stone.

'What's that Mags?'

The clapping wings of a pair of woodpigeons bursting out from the thicket startled them both. Maggie stared after the birds until they were out of sight, then she sighed and tilted her wrist for him to see.

'Should I give it back?'

'Where did you get this?' he asked, although he already knew. A gift, a keepsake, he recognized it at once. The sun seemed to sink suddenly behind the bank of cloud on the horizon, sending them into a deep shade. A crucifix with a Celtic design, blackened with tarnish and filth, the silver shining through where Maggie had rubbed it. The little insects haloed his head. He reached out to touch the crucifix, brush his fingers across it. Maggie's hand was trembling.

'I could give it back,' she said in a near-whisper, 'like you said about the swords and rings. But they gave it to me.'

It was cold to the touch, black against the white palm of his little girl. Cross her palm and hope to. . . Chris had never been without it. For Hamish it was at once around Chris's neck and in Maggie's hand. The cries of rooks and jackdaws, crows and magpies, rose up from the woods in a dissonant frenzy. Chris was out there, beyond the trees in the watery dark. He knew.

Nothing Else Matters

Nicholas Royle

TAKE YOUR GLASSES OFF TO WIPE YOUR EYES AND everything in the distance loses definition. What is that down there? Right at the end. A snooker table? It looks a lot like one. Bright lights suspended over green baize, clink of ball against ball. Oh look, that could be me, sitting close to the table, wearing an old jacket that's two sizes too big and watching a tall, slender young man move around the table, sizing up shots, working out angles. A few weeks from his eighteenth birthday, Joe should be revising for his A-levels, not playing snooker with his dad. He took some persuading, although not because he thought he should be revising. He's bright, bright enough to know what work ethic means, but that's as far as it goes. His mum and I worry about him, always have done. A fortnight ago she told me he wanted to go to a funeral and could I give him a lift? His friend Eddie, not a close friend, but still. Suicide.

'Joe,' I say, 'you're not using the chalk. Use the chalk.'

He screws up his face, curls his lip. His standard look for unwanted advice. But he picks up the chalk and chalks the end of his cue. His granddad's cue, I should say. Loosely between my fingers, as I wait for the chance to come to the table, I hold my own cue, which my dad bought me when I was Joe's age.

'What happened?' I asked Joe as I drove him to Eddie's funeral.

'Dunno. He kind of withdrew over the last few months.'

'What did he…? I mean how…?'

'Overdose.'

I wondered about that word. Wasn't it what a professional might say? I wondered if this was what Eddie's parents said when anyone asked. *He took an overdose.* I wondered how they must be feeling, but shut down that line of enquiry pretty quickly.

I watch Joe stretch across the table to play a shot, one of his size 11 trainers planted on the floor, the other raised behind him, his leg straight as a rapier in baggy jogging pants. On his top half he's wearing one of my 90s long-sleeved T-shirts, which fits him better than it ever fitted me. Gone is the gangly awkwardness of youth, replaced by a fluid agility, latent strength, elegance. He handles my dad's cue with relaxed confidence. Now I know he can play – though I wonder when and where he learned – I'll tell him the cue is his to keep. I wonder if he's been watching the action from the Crucible on his laptop in his bedroom. It would make a change from Facebook or *Game of Thrones*. I wonder if other parents see more of their teenage children than I do of mine, or if they all stay holed up in their bedrooms.

When I picked him up after the funeral I asked how it had gone.

'Good.'

It seemed a strange word to use.

'Did you meet his parents? How were they?'

'Yeah. They were fine. His dad seemed quite cheerful.'

This made me wonder if Joe knew what was at stake, if

he was able to empathise. If he thought Eddie's parents were 'fine' and Eddie's dad's cheerfulness anything other than a mask, might that mean he would be more likely to follow Eddie's example if some impulse told him to? Like I said, his mum and I have always worried.

He was staying at my place that night. After he went out, to the pub – it was a school night, but I guessed it counted as an exception, provided he was meeting a couple of mates to share memories of Eddie and not sitting on his own with a couple of pints – I wandered into his bedroom to pick up his clothes and generally tidy up and there on his bedside cabinet I saw the order of service for Eddie's funeral with what must have been a recent photograph of him on the front. Clear complexion, side-parted blond hair, a faintly disbelieving look in his eyes and an ambiguous half-smile, as if he'd just been told a bad joke. Inside I found the words to a hymn I didn't know, a psalm, a poem ('So Go and Run Free'), a reading by Eddie's dad, more prayers, recessional music by an artist I hadn't heard of. On the back, an invitation to join the family for refreshments. Donations, if desired, to Young Minds: Child and Adolescent Mental Health.

Joe is straighter on the black than he would have liked and will have to screw back hard to get on the red near the middle pocket.

'Shot,' I say, knocking twice on the floor with the butt of my cue.

Joe frowns. It's still a difficult shot into the middle, but he's steadily building up a decent break. I remember when my dad used to take me to the Chorlton Snooker Centre, neither of us could put together much of a sequence. A red and a colour – any colour – was about the limit.

He pockets the red and drops nicely on the blue.

I work out that when my dad and I used to play, he was only ten or eleven years from the end of his life. We probably only went once or twice; my mum doesn't remember us going at all. 'Your dad would never have taken you there,' she insisted the other day. 'You signed the pledge, didn't you?' I said. 'Did you know the Chorlton Snooker Centre used to be the Temperance Billiards Hall?' But I remember him, as clear as day, standing in the half-light of the snooker hall, removing the jacket I'm wearing today and placing it on the nearest bench. He was my height, but stockier.

It's a good job Joe is keeping score. Left alone, he will sometimes get on with things. He's fiercely independent, except when it comes to loading a dishwasher or boiling a kettle. Would he take his parents' advice over exam revision, A-level choices, university applications? He would not. As a consequence he accepted only one offer, which is dependent on grades he's not predicted to achieve. Do we worry? Yes, his mum worries. I worry. Even my partner worries. I daresay his mum's partner worries, too.

I said to his mum the day after Eddie's funeral, 'Something like this puts things into perspective. We both know we worry about him. We've always worried about him. But at least he's healthy and happy. Nothing else matters.'

And if it were really the case, that my son was healthy and happy, nothing else would matter. But the vivid green of the baize is fading, the clink of the balls changing timbre. Doesn't it actually sound more like someone collecting empty glasses in a pub? Maybe a pub that was once a Temperance Billiards Hall and became a snooker club and now doesn't even have a pool table. The kind of pub where middle-aged men buy two pints when they visit the bar, then sit on their own at little round tables, sneaking occasional bites from sandwiches in paper bags. The kind of pub where you might go to sit and wonder what it must feel like to have your worries in perspective. What it must feel like to be the father of one of the boys at Eddie's funeral. A boy like Joe, perhaps. What it must feel like to be Joe's dad and not Eddie's.

The Dandhiyas

Nikesh Shukla

I DON'T WANT YOU TO EVER FEAR SPEAKING UP FOR YOUR people.

My daily anxiety is that your default cultural immersion is to be white. That's the world you're growing up into, with its default language, formalities, relationships and attitudes to mealtimes. It's up to me to ensure you don't ignore that part of you that makes you what people will refer to as other, or different, or, at worst, exotic. It's what makes you a god.

I think this staring at the wall of your cousin's bedroom. You're snoozing. In your car seat. Holding on to Maple. Oblivious to my nervous shifting on the loose floorboards. I came upstairs to check you were okay. As a break from the ebullience of the white half of your family. The sun is out so they are joyfully taking in as much sunshine and al fresco mealtime as they can muster before the clouds come.

On the wall of your cousin's bedroom is a photo of the whole family. It's encased in a makeshift frame that looks familiar. It takes me a full second to recognise the sticks. Strung together into a rectangle are four dandhiyas. Your mother and I gave pairs of them out at our wedding. Now, useless for dance, away from the context of garba and Navratri and our wedding, they've been refashioned into something static.

I feel humiliated looking at them.

I try to find comparisons. It would be like using a crucifix as a bottle opener, is the closest I can come to. We perform garbas in praise of Durga. I'm not religious. We imitate Krishna's playfulness, for he is the Lord of the Dance. Still, I'm not religious. To my sister-in-law, they're pretty sticks that remind the family of a nice occasion. To her, this is repurposing the pretty sticks into something sentimental so that they retain a reverence over the family. They were brought into the family. Now they frame the family.

My job feels harder looking at them, my heart feels heavy with the betrayal.

I have to explain to you why this is not okay, why cultural misappropriation will follow you your entire life. For a while, you'll indulge it because the goofy enthusiasm of some white people means they mean well, even if they're undercutting millennia of tradition just for the opportunity to wear a bindi to a club. Confusingly, it'd be okay for you to do it. Not for them. Never. Well, sometimes it would be okay. That's the complexity of context, you see.

I stand there, and I watch you, and I try to see the world from your eyes, rather than place all my fight and fatigue, my moral compass and my sadness that the most dangerous forms of racism are the seemingly harmless socially acceptable ones, on to your shoulders. You'll be told many times in your lifetime that your skin tone is utterly beautiful. You're so lucky, they'll tell you. You must tan so beautifully. So easily. You're tanned all year round. You're so exotic. So much better than me. I'm so pasty. Until I cook myself in the sun. Just to be as dark as you. We'll know the truth though. Tans fade. You'll never be fully white.

You will become overly familiar with the wrists of friends and colleagues every summer as they compare their skin tones with you.

I was once walking through the centre of our city and a charity man, standing there in his dreadlocks, signing people's email addresses up to social media campaigns, stopped me by saying Here comes the man with the best tan in Bristol. Been anywhere nice? He said. This is my skin tone, I replied. I woke up like this. You must feel so lucky, he told me, as I walked off.

You will always wake up the colour you were born into. Whether you decide to pass for one ethnicity or another, you will always know, in the first few seconds of the day, who you're supposed to be.

Your expertise will be called upon at every Indian restaurant. Especially the types that have the exact same menu. All the Joshs, the Jalfrezis, Pasandas, Tikka Masalas. The dishes invented in the UK for the British palette. People will defer to you. What's good here, they'll ask. Like you know what exactly to order off-menu. I like it spicy, but not too spicy. What's mild but also has a kick to it? There will always be one who wants to order the hottest thing on the menu, because they conflate spiciness with tastiness and they want people to know how amazing they are.

You'll be asked where to get cheap bindis and mehndi. People won't know the difference, because they're actually asking for helping sourcing chandlos and henna.

You'll be asked how to put on a saree correctly, a saree found in a charity shop.

You have all these burdens to come.

What are they saying? They will ask when a bhangra tune comes on. Like you, a half-Gujarati, are an expert in Punjabi slang. People will conflate Asia with Bangladesh with Pakistan with Nepal with Sri Lanka and call it Indian. Like Indian Summers. A clunky term, referring to Native Americans, warm climates after hard frosts and the West. Nothing to do with the country of Asia.

Yes, I said country. Asia and India are interchangeable ways to describe the whole of India, Pakistan, Nepal, Sri Lanka, Bangladesh, South India and more.

You have all these burdens to come.

You will have to sit still at family events, on both sides, sadly (your Gujarati side has been here too long to remember how it felt to not feel like you were wanted here) when they spit and swear about immigrants. You will have to speak for all of your people and none of them. You will have to remain quiet when you see bastardised remnants of a culture half your grandparents' parents migrated from India to Africa to the suburbs of London. You will be the filtration device. You will be like a squash, concentrated flavour, add water to dilute.

I want to rip the dandhiyas off the wall and break them over my knees. These ones are foil laminated over thin malleable metal. I want to throw them in the bin and burn this house down. I feel incensed.

I have so much to teach you.

Sadly, what I have to teach you is armoury.

This is not a way to live your life.

*

I wait for my breakfast sandwich to be barbecued.

Was she okay?, your mother asks. You took ages.

Yes, fine. I got lost for a second. She looks adorable when

she's fast asleep.

People aww.

Such a proud dad, your aunt tells into the air.

The bar for fathers is depressingly low. The kudos I get for basic nurture, care and affection for you is bewildering.

Changing a shitty nappy is not special.

Spending time with you is not special (well, it is special, but the act of it is not).

Putting you to bed every other night, getting up to calm and soothe you if you wake, even when I had work the next day and your mother was still on maternity leave, was not special.

Why am I a saint and she a mother?

I had it easy those early months. I got to go to work. I got to have adult conversations. I had to shower. I got to choose what to have for my lunch. I got to have a break in order to eat my lunch. I got to leave you and come back for you. I got to live your mother's worst fears and frustrations through text. I got to see pictures of you at your best over text.

I then came home. And you were handed to me immediately. Your mother had had enough.

I never had enough.

Such a proud dad, I think. What does that even mean?

My father never changed any of my nappies. He chose work. He didn't read me bedtime stories. He didn't cook me a single meal. He let me crawl into bed with him on Saturday and Sunday mornings and snuggle in, even though my mother hated the idea of the children invading her bed, her last safe house, her last bastion of independence.

I end up over-extending, over-compensating, being the opposite of my father. Trying to give you everything he didn't give me. Not because I want to be seen as a proud dad, or a good dad, or be given spurious societal brownie points. I will not deem myself as anything special. I just want you to have all the things I think I lacked. Maybe I can create a better version of myself.

My dad never changed any of my nappies. He has few memories of me or my sister as a baby. He doesn't know what songs were sung to us, what our favourite picture books were or whether we slept or cried through the night.

It must be a generational thing, I figure, for me to want to be so hands-on. To scoop away waste from the birthing pool, to change nappies, to sing songs, to do some of the night time cuddle support. It's now socially acceptable for men to be fathers.

My dad is of a type though. The Gujarati male father figure.

We were never close until my late twenties, when circumstance meant I had to help him financially. We were never close until we worked together and spent lunches together and his pride was replaced with mutual respect. It took us a long time to get to the place where we could converse beyond perfunctory updates on career and housing and sport, mostly cricket. I don't want my child to get to know me late in life. I want her to know me from the start.

I will not wake up to a cup of tea made for me in silence while I cough up my lungs and clear my sinuses of thick phlegm. I will not change the channel from whatever frivolity is on one channel in order to watch the news and check Ceefax for the cricket updates on another. I will not work till late at night, come home and drink, staring into space thinking about work, engaging my children only to nod and reprimand as required. I will not eat my meals by myself, one hand clutching the plate, the other shovelling food into my mouth as quickly as possible as I watch half an hour of television and count the seconds till my night cap. I will not work on weekends. I will not avoid changing nappies. I will not only be concerned with exam results and studies. I will not only take an interest at defined junctures. I will not lose sight of the everyday of my children.

I will not be my father.

I respect the man. I will be the opposite of him.

I eat my barbecued breakfast bacon sandwich and I walk inside to check on you.

Awww, I hear on my footsteps. What a concerned proud father.

*

You're still sleeping. I stand in front of the dandhiya frame. The photo is stuck to the wall. The dandhiyas dangle, limply, loosely capturing the image.

I take them off the wall and hold them. The foil is coming off with the clam of my hands. I undo the string that binds these dandhiyas together in a square and place them in pairs, one crossing the other, on the bed. I look at them and smile at the memory.

We had all of our guests line up at our wedding. We had these dandhiyas given to us for free, wedding favours left over from a cousin's wedding, where they had obviously expected over a hundred more guests than came.

Our family is big. Overwhelming. Shrill. It talks in another language. The chips are stacked against us.

I watched as my sister shouted out instructions over a megaphone on how to do the dandhiya ras. People stiffly copied the instructions. Your mother and I stood at the end of the line watching the chaos, thinking it was the funniest thing we had ever seen. You have to understand something to subvert it. It has to be part of you.

You'll find in the future that non-black rap fans are obsessed with wanting to say the n-word. They can't. They will kick and scream for the right. They will semanticise and argue and debate for the right. It is not their word to reclaim, throw around flippantly or use with any intent other than offense. Finally, they'll say, but black people say it. Why can't we?

You'll see your friends wanting to borrow your bindis. For fashion. And part of you will see it as harmless fun. They're just bindis. It's just fashion. It's okay.

The puppetry of fashion, blindly attacking the surface of everything with the obsessive need to look cool. What happens when we're out of vogue? What then? Who are we and what do our bindis mean when they're last season? What of the bindis that let people call our sisters, aunts, mothers and grandmas 'dotheads'? When we walked into rooms and people asked who farted, or demanded to know where the curry stink came from? Bud-bud-bud-bud went our oscillating heads and voices. Where were those bindis then? It's never harmless.

At a reading last week, a woman approached me afterwards. She waited till I looked like I'd broken whatever deep thought I was in and pounced. I knew she was waiting for me. I had seen her looking at me with an intensity that meant she thought she was looking into my soul, with her third eye, during my reading. Everyone else looked at me, at their phones, their feet, the ceiling, the other people on the stage, some even closed their eyes – they politely gave me the eyeball time they thought I deserved. She kept my eyeline at all times, I lost my place on the page three or four times because of the sheer intensity emanating from her. She was blonde, had a tan mark in the middle of her eyebrows, which made me think she'd been wearing a bindi in the sun, she had open-toed sandals on, no nail varnish, and a long flowing skirt, somewhere between tie-dye and sequins. Her blonde hair had volume, stature, like she was rich enough to have the time to blowdry every single day. I wasn't talking to anyone. I was doing everything to avoid talking to anyone. That way I could remember I was, outside of this elevated situation, and go home to my wife and child remembering my place in the world. Your work, she told me. It reminds me all of the yoga retreats in India I've been to.

This is the world I've brought you into.

*

A week later, I'm walking around New York.

I've been waiting for this trip for four months. Four months of my old life. Of drinking, talking frivolous bullshit, looking at things to buy for myself in shops, smoking, dancing – everything you've stopped me from doing. I'll rephrase. Everything I decided wasn't as good as spending time with you.

I've fetishised the trip.

I'm here and I ensure my walks take me past as many Starbucks as possible. So I can Whatsapp your mum for a rolling stream of information about you. So I can Facetime you and see the initial smile and shy nose-picking before you get embarrassed and weirded out by my disembodied head on a screen and walk away. So I can tell your mother how much I can't wait to come home.

It's unhelpful.

She's made peace with the trip. Why haven't I?

I realise my life has changed.

And I'm back in that bedroom again, watching you sleep, angry at four sticks on the wall.

I stop in front of a coffee shop offering free Wi-Fi, sign in and sent a Facetime request. Your mum accepts and we connect. You're in shot, chewing on your finger, staring at the screen because you've been told to look at the screen. New Yorkers walk past me. I am five hours behind you, in the city I long to be in most days.

Daddy kya che? I ask, the only Gujarati sentence you know. You look at the screen with fresh eyes. You smile, with recognition and point at me. I ask her how you are. Interacting with you causes you to get shy, upset; it breaks the communication and you walk out of screen. Your mum appears and gives me a brief update of the you and the your day.

I nod, and I feel far away.

I see your hands make it into shot. You look darker than I remember. I realise I've become that person I want you to arm yourself against. It's just skin tone. It's not who you are.

I long to be home, I say.

Your mum knows.

I better go, I say. Ow-jho, I say to you. Jay Shree Krishna, I repeat, as is custom, like I am teaching you.

You say die-die, which we know means goodbye.

I remember, early on, I talked to you a lot more in Gujarati. You laughed. You giggled. You found it hilarious. I said to your mum that I worried you thought Gujarati was gibberish.

Maybe she's just racist, I joke.

We talk about your cultural heritage. How I was concerned that you will grow up without the ability to speak Gujarati, any knowledge of Hinduism, no chilli tastebuds and your ears will be a Bollywood-free zone. It's up to me to educate you. In things, your mum said. These are things. That are products of a culture, not an understanding of it. The default is English, I continued. Everything in her life is English. It's up to me to enforce the Indian part. I just don't know how to, because I shied away from it so much. It's like, we have a milk chocolate bar in front of us. And currently, the mixture is too milky. We need to add more dark chocolate into the mix. Milky milk chocolate is the worst.

It sounds like you're racist, your mum said. Against chocolate.

Sometimes I forget how wise she is.

I hope you take after her.

Apple

Richard W. Strachan

T HE WIDE, PINK MOON-FACE STUDDED IN THE CENTRE BY its gestural trio of mouth and eyes, and the eyes making a coy sidelong glance to meet his own as he crawled around to see her, Apple gazed up at him from the shadowed crook between the sofa and the edge of the bookcase. The tapering jester's hat, its terminal bell long since near-swallowed and thrown away, was covered in a furry tangle of cobweb and dust. Poor Apple, he thought, and he was surprised at the thickening that came to his throat. Apple, the soft smile still moulded on her cinnamon-scented face, had been bent and stuffed down as far as a five-year-old arm could reach, the cloth body flowing easily into the gap. He thought of the absurd voice he sometimes used to animate the thing for his daughter's amusement, and he used it now as he reached down to pull her free.

Mama! he squeaked. *Mama did this to Apple!*

The end of the hat, where the bell had come away (that bell! Herald of the somnolent midnight visit, tolling mightily on the borders of his sleep – if Rowan had not bitten it off he would in time have chucked it out himself) was frayed and still damp from his daughter's ministrations. Last night this thing was still loved. The stumpy cloth arms were grey with dirt and greasy with emollient cream, and the cheery pink floral dress was unravelling at the hem. All signs of a child's deep and abiding affection.

He held the doll, which was head to toe not much bigger than the span of fingertip to wrist, and called for his daughter.

Rowan, he shouted. He assumed his parental authority. Can you come here please.

The child came into the room, clutching Apple's replacement – Rose, the more robust and realistic doll he had bought for her that morning. It was nothing like this abstract thing he held in his hand; Apple, the cave painting to Rose's photo-real portrait.

What's this? I found Apple down the back of the sofa?

Rowan said nothing. She looked up at him through her straggling hair – that damned hair clip, he would never get it right. She clutched Rose under one arm; the new doll, it was the best he could do.

He handed Apple to her, and with a look on her face of cold and adult contempt, she slipped past him to stuff the doll back into her prison behind the sofa. She looked at him not with defiance but with an unmoved expectation of the protest she knew was about to follow.

What on earth are you doing that for? Poor Apple, he said. Poor, poor Apple…

He started crying in the Apple-tone, and when he pulled her back out and offered her to Rowan, the child, making it all now completely unambiguous, punched the doll in her plastic face and sent her falling from his hand.

There was no point taking it any further. He knew that from experience. He looked at the grim line of his daughter's mouth, the hooded eyes, and told her in a stern voice that she shouldn't treat her toys so badly. There was no point even sending her to her room, but ten minutes later he could hear her through there, putting Rose to bed, laying her out under the blanket that had once belonged to Apple, setting under her head the little embroidered pillow Rowan's grandmother had made for her when she was a baby.

Poor, poor Apple... He recovered the doll once more, grubby and sordid, and brushed off the cobwebs. Reflexively he raised it to his face, inhaling the faint and lingering trace of cinnamon from the plastic.

Bad mama! he said quietly, to the quiet house. *I am so sad.*

*

They had bought Apple for her when she was potty-training, a successful bribe to get her over those first, inhibiting traumas. Apple, the name, had been Rowan's suggestion. *The face looks like something you could bite!* she had said, and to this day you could still see the mild indentations where her teeth had made good on the observation. After that, Apple, 'her baby', was never out of her grasp, at least while she was in the house. Instinctively they knew that the doll was too valuable to risk taking it outside; he could well imagine the screaming meltdown, the red-faced grief if her baby was ever lost. Whenever Rowan was at nursery or they had gone out for the day, Apple's wide pink face would loom over the cusp of her baby blanket in the space beside Rowan's bed, safely tucked up until she came home. Rowan slept with her, ate breakfast, lunch and dinner with her, and included her not so much as another toy, but as an active participant in her games. He would make up little stories about Apple to entertain her, reciting them as if from Apple's mouth in that ludicrous, high-pitched baby voice, dangling the doll by the tip of her hat and making her skip and gambol around Rowan's bedroom, naughtily scampering up the bunk-bed's posts to the top mattress. All this seemed to layer the ridiculous little doll with another dimension of reality in Rowan's eyes, and sometimes he even caught himself meeting that sidelong gaze and seeing in the painted eyes something like a look of thanks, for imbuing her with this kind of life.

But now, after everything else, all that ardour and devotion had been transferred. Apple's stock had fallen in the gutter, never to be picked up again. Rose had definitively replaced her.

He tried to reintroduce the doll as quickly as possible; the longer she dwelled in disfavour, he supposed, the harder it would be for Rowan to accept her again, like a chick reintroduced to the nest after a night on the ground. At bedtime he briskly tucked Apple under the covers next to Rowan, the tip of her hat dry now for what was probably the first time in almost three years. Rowan turned her back.

The next morning (and it was practically the first thing he thought of) he checked the bed, but there was no sign of Apple. He sat opposite his daughter at the kitchen table as she parsed her cornflakes, Rose slumped awkwardly on the chair beside her.

Where's Apple? he asked.

She shrugged and continued eating.

Rowan, can you look at me please? Tell me, what have you done with Apple? Where is she?

I don't know daddy.

He got her off to school, at the gate meeting none of

the other parents' eyes, radiating what he hoped was an unmistakable desire for silence. He clutched Rowan when the bell went, pressing his lips to her warm forehead and watching her gallop across the playground to the school doors. When he got back home he stood in the doorway of her bedroom and listened to the empty house, its dormancy, hearing above the tick of wainscot and the buzzing of the fridge the cool drift of traffic on the main road, the birds chattering from the trees that shielded the park. He could hear the liquid beating of his heart and he placed his hand against it.

Later, he spent an hour searching for the doll, interrogating all the nooks and crannies in the house. He came up with nothing in Rowan's bedroom. He searched through her bedclothes and under her bed, through all her drawers and boxes and bags and bits, and although he found any number of Lego pieces and plastic oddments, he couldn't find Apple at all. He searched in his own bedroom, even rifling through those plastic bags of clothes that he still had to take to the charity shop, but Apple wasn't there either. It was only much later in the afternoon, not long before he was due to collect his daughter from school, an afternoon that had bled away from him as leisurely as the autumn sky had bled itself of light, that he found the doll in the kitchen bin. Emptying out some coffee grounds, he looked and there she was, face down like a body in the tide, half covered with cabbage leaves and paper.

She must have done it while he was asleep, during the night. He was beginning to suspect this anyway. The night terrors were over, but he was sure that she was getting up still stunned in half sleep and wandering around the house, confused, forgetting what had happened. He found the photographs in odd positions sometimes, in the mornings, some of those ornaments disarranged. It must be her, unless he was losing his mind – not outside the realms of possibility. He tried to picture her stepping on her light bare feet through the darkened hallways; he tried to imagine the range of the questions that might suggest themselves to her, and which she wasn't able to articulate, even to herself. Some intimation of that child's mind, the half-remembered shape of its intuitions, came back to him as he stood there in the kitchen with the filthy doll in his hands, and for a moment it was overwhelming.

He put Apple in the washing machine and went out to collect his daughter.

*

He didn't say anything about it that night. He hung Apple up to dry and tucked his daughter in to bed, reading her stories while she hugged Rose tightly, but he said nothing.

The next morning, after Rowan had ceremoniously put Rose to bed and got herself ready for school, he came into her bedroom with Apple and laid the doll carefully on the empty top bunk. Rowan watched him with wary interest. He took a hand towel from the bathroom and used it as a blanket, and leaning over he kissed Apple goodbye before he took Rowan to school.

She made no mention of it as they walked in, and when he brought her home she didn't make the expected dash to her bedroom to tip the interloper to the floor. Still, when he put her to bed that night, there was again no sign of Apple.

The punishment wasn't too severe this time - she'd just been thrown into a corner of the room - but the bed had been desecrated; the sheet hauled out, the towel cast to the foot of the mattress and the pillow who knew where.

Why are you doing this? he demanded, and when Rowan gave him that indifferent shrug (a terrifying glimpse, he thought, of the teenager who was trapped inside) he felt a rush of fury that had him slamming his way out of the room and sitting on the edge of his bed until the blood had dimmed its tide in his veins. He sat there and cradled Apple in his lap; the soft sobbing came from the back of his throat, the wavering baby voice lamenting its lot. *Oh why, mama, why!*

There was no real strategy to it, no psychological cut and thrust, but getting Rowan to accept what she had rejected now became the guiding struggle of his days.

They had hectic, circular arguments where he tried to drag the truth from her, constantly questioning and wheedling and hammering out the facts until Rowan's face was a bewildered mask of snot and tears, which he dismissed from the table with an angry wave. He forced Apple into her hands, bending her fingers around the doll's pliable leg, threatening her with terrible sanctions or bribing her with promises of chocolate and cake. He even took Rose from her, like some fairy tale villain bundling the doll up while she slept, spiriting it away to a hiding place in the cupboard under the stairs, and placing Apple like a changeling in Rowan's outstretched, sleeping arms. If he hoped for a simple transfer of affection though, he was disappointed, and her distress the next morning was genuine enough for him to relent. Rose was disinterred, resurrected.

It was a question of wills, he thought. Her intransigence was coming up against his own, and his would prevail. It was this stubbornness in the face of what was best for her that exasperated him most. It was infuriating, and it was more than the idea of the doll or the sentiment that he had tacked on to it that moved him. I just want what's best for her, he thought. That's it, just what's best, in her own best interests, just to see her happy and safe, even if she doesn't understand why.

And she had had Apple for so long, since she was a baby practically, and it was such a shame - it lodged there in his throat, all the happy, indigestible past. Why was she doing this. She would regret it for the rest of her life. Can one thing just go right, just one?

Every morning he took her to school, and every afternoon he collected her and brought her home, and all his time in between he spent in dedicated service to Apple. He took needle and thread and repaired the ragged hem of her dress. He polished the disc of her plastic face, and used cinnamon oil to freshen the scent. He even fixed a new bell to the tip of the hat, and hand washed her until the limbs were as spruce as they had been in the box, when they had first bought her. Then, taking an indirect route through the thickets of reverse psychology, he placed this new improved Apple high up on a bookshelf in a prominent position, where Rowan couldn't fail to see her. She was directly in her eyeline when they sat down to dinner, and as they ate he watched with satisfaction as her gaze flicked up to the space behind him, again and again. It was with a sense of a great and perfectly orchestrated plan slotting finally into position that he answered Rowan's request to take Apple down with a firm and resonant 'No.'

Why? she said.

You have Rose now, don't you? You don't need Apple anymore. And, he added, Apple doesn't need you.

No mama! he said in the baby voice, a dart of real anguish stabbing in his gut at the sight of Rowan's equally anguished expression. *Me don't like you anymore!* And that night he made a show of placing Apple in his own room, safely tucked up in his own bed, and he promised her in Rowan's hearing that he would make sure she was cuddled all night.

*

He came awake, a fast unravelling, and reached in the dark for the other side of the bed. Even Apple wasn't there. As his eyesight settled in the lighter gloom he saw a slice of night-light bleeding from the hall, through the crack of his part-open door.

A sound next, the sense of a presence awake and walking. He almost called out her name. He could see a dark, bulky shape across the room, but it was only those plastic bags, the clothes for the charity shop. He must take them. He could see himself for the first time taking them in, and then getting back to work. There was so much to be done. He had to get back to himself, for Rowan.

In the hall he stood and listened. The night light's lunar glow laid a streak of silver across the carpet, a path he followed to the head of the stairs.

Rowan?

She was down in the kitchen. He peered around the door and saw her there, sitting at the table with Apple resting in her lap, the photographs in their frames laid out in front of her. She held one up and glanced it over, passing on to the next, then the next. He called her name again but she didn't answer, and when he crossed the room quietly and looked into her face he could see that some part of her was still deeply asleep. She barely knew what she was doing. Instinct, maybe. The presence of a loss that woke her in the nights, now no more with screaming but with this sense of seeking out. He thanked God that the screaming fits had stopped, all those nights he had felt like screaming himself.

He lifted her up and carried her back to her room. She wouldn't remember any of this in the morning. She held Apple by her jester's hat, the tinkling sound of the little bell following them up the stairs.

Time for bed mama, he said. *Time for mama and baby to go to bed.*

When she was at school the next day he took Rose, discarded now, and put her in the bag with the other toys. He drove them all away, the clothes too, and when he came back he stopped outside the house as if seeing it for the first time, this new place where they both would live.

=VLOOKUP

(E2,'[Turnover year end 2015.xlsQ1SalesLeads'!$E$2:$F$1001,2,0

Richard V. Hirst

H IS TYPING IS INTERRUPTED BY HIS PHONE BUZZING IN HIS
pocket. He takes it out, sees that it is his wife calling him
then slips it back into his pocket. He places his hands back
over his keyboard, closes his eyes and focuses on the sounds
beyond his booth – the photocopier on the other side of his
partition wall, the quiet chatter in the rest of the office, the
hushed traffic moving through the streets outside – whilst
he waits for the buzzing to stop. Then he resumes typing,
completing the formula.

His job is research. He finds business contacts for the
company's sales department, investigates them and assesses
their value. He has the basics in front of him, the profit and
turnover of the individuals' companies, their salaries and
the numbers of staff under them, their areas of expenditure:
the usual. He is almost done. But he has some additional
information which he thinks will impress Malcolm.
Information on the strongest competitors of his current list
of contacts: like-for-like figures on people in similar roles in
similar companies in similar sectors. Similar, but similar is
not identical.

He stares at his spreadsheet. Almost done, but not quite. He has had an idea. He could look at the ages of the individuals he is researching, then compare the patterns of their behaviour to other professionals in their age-ranges. He could do a great number of things. There is a great deal of information he could find which would help Sales build strong relationships and which–

His phone buzzes again and then stops again. It does this a further three times. Each time, he stops his work, shuts his eyes and listens to the sounds of the office around him.

*

Carol is sitting up in bed, her iPad propped on her lap, a near-empty glass of wine in her hand.

'Sorry,' he says, taking off his jacket, hanging it up. 'It was insane at the office.'

She says: 'I tried to phone you earlier.'

'Oh, right?' He steps out of his shoes, pulls off his tie. 'Sorry. I've not had a chance to even look at my phone, I don't think. It was absolute bedlam.'

'Zak got into a fight. They phoned me.'

'A fight?'

'He didn't start it, didn't even fight back, they said. I had to go in and pick him up. He was in a right state.'

'What happened?'

'He's got a nasty-looking bruise across one eye. And a cut on his forehead, not as bad as it looks. I took him to A&E.'

'Oh god, is he okay?'

'I tried phoning you.'

'Is he alright?'

'He'll be fine.'

'Do we know who did it?'

'You remember Yvo?'

'Is he in one of the years above?'

'No, Yvo. Yvo Hamley. A she. She's in Zak's year. Dark, curly hair, noisy, tall. Her mother's American. Does something weird. Makes music videos or something.'

'And she hit him?'

'Beat him up. They told me she'll be suspended tomorrow. Probably get excluded, they reckon.'

'And he didn't fight back at all?'

'That's what they told me.'

*

They are both at the kitchen table, his wife is in her pyjamas, Zak in his school uniform, eating cereal, a bruised eye on the television on the other side of the room. Outside, beyond the window, it is still dark, dawn just beginning.

'Morning, killer,' he says and laughs.

Zak doesn't respond, goes on chewing.

'You want coffee?' his wife asks.

He looks at his watch. 'We should be making tracks, to be honest.'

'Early,' she says.

'I'll drop you off at Donnie's, okay?' he says.

'Do I have to?' says Zak.

'Does he have to?' says Carol.

'It's best if I get in before everyone else. Gives me a chance to get some actual work done before the mayhem begins.'

*

In the car, after a few minutes of listening to the radio, he says: 'Do you want to talk to me about what happened?'

'Nothing happened,' says Zak.

'Well, something happened.'

Zak sighs. 'She just started hitting me. I didn't even see what happened. I was coming out of science and she was hiding outside the door. She jumped out and started, like, hitting me.'

'But why? Why did she hit you?'

'I don't know.'

'Are you sure you hadn't done anything? You didn't say anything or give her a funny look or anything like that?'

'No,' Zak says and turns to look out of the window. 'I went through all of this with mum already, and Mrs. Jong.'

'Well, don't worry about today. Yvo won't be there. Maybe for good, if I speak to Mrs. Jong. Would you like that?'

'I don't know.'

'Or I could go and speak to Yvo's mum.'

'I don't know. It'd feel a bit weird.'

'That's true,' he says, stopping the car. 'You should fight your own fights. That's a good point.'

Zak gets out, trudges up the long, dim driveway toward Donnie's house and rings the doorbell.

*

He spends the morning Googling and then adding into the spreadsheet the ages of each of the businessmen he is researching. While looking up this information he also discovers other things about them: some are on the boards of charities, others donate to political parties; some were born in the areas their companies are based, others have moved; some are privately educated, others at state comprehensives; most are married but some are not; some have daughters, some sons, others no children; some have grandchildren; one is gay; some have illnesses, or partners with illnesses, or children; some are public about their hobbies – motorcars, poker, football – others are not; some have spent time in the army.

All of this could be useful for Sales. He notes down what he learns in a separate spreadsheet – a column of biography on each of the men – then scrolls through what he has, assessing and reassessing, thinking how best this data can be assimilated into his main sheet, how best all of this can be used. He creates a colour code – yellow for old with a traditional family, red for young with a traditional family, blue for old and divorced, green for young and divorced – but then removes the colours. None of them are quite right. Too many details, too much overlap.

He feels his phone buzz in his pocket. He stops typing, shuts his eyes and focuses on the printer, its purring and clicking filling his corner of the room, until the phone stops buzzing. Then he opens his eyes. The light outside, he notices, has grown weak. It is after 3pm. The afternoon has rushed away from him. He stands, stretches, takes his phone out of his pocket, shoves it into the middle of a stack of papers on his desk and leaves the office.

*

The refrigerator shelf hums, near empty. He is too late for a decent lunch. All that are left are a pair of cheap egg and cress sandwiches and a deluxe tuna mayonnaise baguette. He picks up the baguette and a bottle of Coke, then goes to get a packet of crisps.

That's when he sees Yvo. He recognises her instantly. She is dressed in her St Bede's uniform, tall, her curls dark and lurid. She is stood at the opposite end of an aisle, her back to him, her tallness imposing, her face in profile. She is talking with someone obscured from view – he can hear conversation but can't make out the words – then walking, disappearing.

He moves quickly to keep her in sight, pacing past the cakes and biscuits. As he rounds the corner he sees she is accompanied by her mother. The similarities are striking: their heights, their stature, their hair. They are leaving the shop, strolling slowly through the sliding doors, already merging with the school-rush bustle of pedestrians.

Not wanting to lose them, he dashes out onto the street. The darkness is setting in, the streetlights flickering on, low orange all around, a cold paring the air. He moves behind Yvo and her mother, matching their pace, allowing a handful of people to amble in and out of space between them, focusing on them, on the backs of their heads, black beacons amid the jostle.

If there is anger – if Yvo's mother is angry with her daughter for attacking his son and being excluded – it doesn't show. They talk as they move, Yvo speaking, now her mother – he can hear her accent – both of them nodding, now laughing.

And suddenly running. His heart bolts. At a crossing on the main road they both leap from the pavement, dodging through the sluggish traffic. He stops walking, his knees weak, ready to think up his story. There's another inner bolt when he sees that in his hands he is still holding the sandwich and bottle of Coke, unpaid-for.

But their jogging slows as they reach a bus-stop on the other side of the road in time to flag down a bus. He ditches the sandwich and Coke into a bin and follows, sprinting out, shuffling through the cars' bumper-glare and onto the bus. Number 333 – the sign on the front reads *Claverick*. He boards and sees the two of them disappearing up the steps to the upper deck.

He buys a ticket, follows Yvo and her mother up the stairs. He passes them and sits down, leaving an empty seat between him and them. The bus pulls away, moving slowly through the traffic.

He hears Yvo say to her mother, 'Monty threw up in my room again last night.'

'Oh jeez,' her mother says. 'Not again. Seriously?'

'It's because he eats that new food you got him too quickly. Have you seen him? Proper little gannet.'

'What? Gannet, did you say? What's gannet?'

'Just someone who eats too quickly, Mom.'

'Well, that's Monty. It's like he's scared someone's going to steal his food.'

Yvo laughs. They both laugh,

'Did you clean it up?'

'I'll do it when we get home.'

'Jeez Louise, Yvo.'

'I'll do it when I get home.'

They laugh again and then lapse into an uneventful silence, checking their phones, staring out of the windows. The bus remaining largely empty. He stares out of the windows too, watching rows of unfamiliar buildings blur by in the darkness.

They ring the stop bell at a quiet, anonymous suburb: a wide, empty street backgrounded by rows of identical unlit houses. To avoid detection, he decides he will get off at the next stop. He watches them disembark and fleetingly – through his high window, as the bus peels away – sees them turn a corner, pass beneath a streetlight, heading down a street.

He rings the bell, goes downstairs, steps off and, seeing he is alone, jogs back to the previous stop. He finds the street corner: Keith Street. Also empty. He trots down the street, which comes to an end splitting in two directions. He picks the left hand street and wanders down for a few minutes, but, already feeling himself beginning to get lost, turns back. He does the same on the right hand street.

He returns to the main road where he loiters for over an hour before a taxi passes by.

*

It is after 6 o'clock by the time he gets back. The office is quiet: almost everyone else has left; the cleaners move from desk to desk, wiping down phone handsets and picking up empty mugs.

He stares at his spreadsheet for a few minutes, clicking between tabs, looking at the data, thinking about the personal information he has collected. Then he Googles *Yvo Hamley*. Then *Yvo Hamley Claverick*. Then *Yvo Hamley Keith Street Claverick*. Then *Yvo Hamley American*. He finds nothing. He looks up Keith Street on Google Street View: a bright, sunny day, the windows on the street all muted black.

From among the stack of print-offs his phone buzzes: a short single buzz, a text message. He retrieves it from the pile and sees on the screen that it's from his wife. He lets the screen go black then slips it in his pocket.

He must focus on his spreadsheet. He must focus.

*

Carol finds him in the corridor, as he is quietly pulling the front door shut and hanging up his coat. She is moving from room to room, turning out the downstairs lights.

'I was about to try phoning you again.'

'Sorry. It was another hectic day.'

'It's fine.'

'There's so much pressure at the moment. I'm sure it'll be worth it. Malcolm's told me he's really impressed with my work.'

'Have you eaten?' she asks, starting up the stairs.

'I grabbed a sandwich,' he says, following.

In the bedroom she says: 'Mrs. Jong called me in this morning. I texted you about it.'

'Right.'

'Did you see my text?' She sits at her dressing table.

'No, I don't know if I did. Sorry.'

'She told me,' Carol says slowly, taking out her contact lenses, 'that Yvo has been excluded from the school.'

'Excluded? So does that mean for good?'

'Yeah. It's like being expelled. Told me she was getting her things out of the locker as we were speaking.'

'Just like that? For hitting Zak?' He takes off his jacket, his shoes, his tie.

'You make it sound like she just threw a single punch. I know you think she's just a girl, but she beat him up.'

'No, I just meant did she have a history of this sort of thing before?'

'I've no idea.'

'I don't think it's unreasonable to expect our son to not be attacked whilst he's at that school.'

'Well then,' she stands, slips into the bed, picks up her iPad. 'This is good news, isn't it?'

'What's wrong?'

'I don't like that I had to go there on my own again. To the school.'

'There's no way I could get out of work this afternoon. It's a madhouse.'

'They should let you leave if it's an emergency.'

'This wasn't an emergency, was it?'

'You could have told them it was.'

*

In the car Zak yawns and says: 'Why do we have to leave so early?'

'Because I need to get into work early to get loads of boring stuff done.'

'But I'm going to have to sit in Donnie's house for ages.'

'I thought you liked Donnie.'

'I do. But I have to just sit there, watching him eat breakfast. It's a bit weird.'

'It's not weird.'

'He was weird with me yesterday.'

'Really? In what way?'

'I don't know. I think he wanted to make fun of me for being beaten up.'

'Well, you did the right thing. Don't let anyone tell you you didn't stand up for yourself. Hitting a girl is never okay.'

'I didn't hit her, Dad.'

'That's exactly what I'm saying.'

Zak yawns again. He chews a piece of toast he has brought with him. 'Why do we have to leave the house so early?'

*

It's beginning to get light by the time he parks his car on the corner of Keith Street, the traffic thickening. He listens to the radio and watches parents walking with their children, people on their way to their jobs.

At nine fifteen he phones Malcolm.

'Hi Malcolm. It's me. I'm not sure I'll make it in today. It's Zak.'

'Zak?'

'My son. He got into a fight outside school.'

'Oh, is he okay?'

'I'm not sure. I mean, I think so.'

'What, so you need to go pick him up?'

'Yes, as far as I know. His teacher hasn't told me much, but A&E was mentioned.'

'Shit.'

'It's not the first time he's done this, to be honest. I think she wants to nip it in the bud.'

'Is Carol okay?'

'I've not told her about it yet. I'd rather deal with it myself before I do.'

'Yes, quite right. Well – of course. Go. I'll see you tomorrow.'

He puts his phone back into his pocket. He sits and watches and waits.

*

He turns up the radio to listen to a programme about football news. He watches the shrubs and bushes which lean over the front yard walls moving back and forth in a breeze. The football programme comes to an end and is replaced by a discussion about raising children, what it's like to be raised by two gay fathers. He changes the station, listens to Elvis Presley.

It's almost noon when Yvo and her mother appear in his wing-mirror, a pair of distant figures, the smudge of their hair marking them out. He presses the button to lower his window a little and makes a show of checking his phone as they pass by, listening to them speak, laughing and talking over one another. Yvo's mother is saying, 'No, no, no...' whilst laughing, her American accent stretching the syllable out. Yvo, in her British, is saying, 'No, listen to me... it's not what you're thinking,' also laughing. He inhales deeply, as they trail away, his head lilting from side to side, but he can't smell them, can smell only his woodland glade air freshener.

He waits until they're a safe distance ahead, closes his window and then gets out of his car. He walks behind them, his phone in his hand, his look of deep concentration at the ready. They pass a row of indistinguishable terraced houses, take a turn onto a short run of shuttered takeaways, grubby off-licences and a small car dealership, and then more terraces. He wonders how he will find his way back.

At a church they leave the pavement and head into the

graveyard.

'Okey-doke,' says Yvo's mother. 'Class is in session!'

He stops by the entrance gate, watching them move away from him, leaving the gravel path for the grass, wandering through the graves. He continues on the pavement, still able to follow their movements through the railings and leafless perimeter shrubs, but their activities – they appear to have stopped, to be doing something – are obscured.

He comes to a bus-stop, giving him an excuse to stop and stand. He peers through at them. Yvo's mother is perching against a tall gravestone, an arm sprawled up against its marble column. The traffic behind him is sparse but he grows irritated as each car passes by, causing him to break off from craning his neck to pretend to be reading a text message.

Yvo, he can see, is taking photographs of her mother. They move between a handful of headstones. Her mother stands in front of another grave, angles her arms above her, looks at the ground, hitches her leg up against its base. Yvo says to her mother, 'That's great... look up... no, this way... move your arm round... eyes on me, Mom... perfect... the light's great today...'

He turns with a low growl at a bus which pulls up noisily at the stop, the handful of passengers eyeballing him. The doors open and he makes eye-contact briefly with the driver who frowns at him, is about to ask him if he wants to board the bus. He steps back. A woman with a pram struggles to lower it to the pavement, also looking at him, expecting his help. He lifts his phone to his ear, but he can't quite bring himself to pretend he is having a conversation. He is waiting for someone to pick up. 'Come on, come on,' he mutters, shaking his head. He turns, making sure the outlines of Yvo and her mother are still there.

Eventually the bus moves away and the woman wheels her pram in the opposite direction. He returns to peeking through at the churchyard and, as he does so, a third figure intrudes on the scene. An elderly man is striding along the path by the graves Yvo and her mother are using, appears to be moving into position for his own photograph. But then the old man passes a gap in the overgrown bramble, becomes visible and he sees he's a stranger. He doesn't know them, is merely visiting a grave. He thinks he even hears him tut.

They leave, Yvo and her mother. Yvo throws something at the man. He can't see what it is. He thinks it might be a grave vase. Whatever it is, it misses the man, scattering noisily into the walkway a few feet from him. It's not clear if he even notices.

'Yvo!' says her mother, 'Jeez.' He hears Yvo giggle.

Slowly, Yvo's mother passes by the gap in the bramble. It is his first proper opportunity to look at her. He moves his eyes across her hair, her eyes, her nose, her lips. Greedily, hungrily. A gannet.

*

Their house, he learns, is on the street where he has parked, on the corner. Once they go inside he gets into his car and moves it to the front of their house.

He sits, watching. But there is no movement. The curtains are shut but the day is still bright and the lights won't need to be turned on for a few hours.

*

'Jesus,' says Carol, flopping onto her back. 'Where did that come from?'

'I know.' He drops down beside her. 'I have no idea.'

They lie alongside one another for a moment. Then she laughs. She takes a breath. She sits up and gathers her clothes from the floor by the bed. He watches her sift through them: her blouse with the popped-off buttons, bra with an irrevocably stretched strap, her torn knickers.

'Ruined,' she says and laughs again. 'All of them.'

'Sorry. I've no idea where that even came from.'

Silence for a while. They catch their breath.

'Do you think we could do something tomorrow?' Carol says. 'You could call in sick.'

'Do something?'

'We could stay in bed all day. I mean, we'd have to be out of the house when the cleaners come at three. But we could go out somewhere. We could go to the cinema.'

'Yeah. That sounds nice. Maybe next week.'

*

'How's Alfie?'

'Alfie?'

'Your boy? Alfie's his name, isn't it?'

'My son. Yes.'

'Everything alright with the school?'

'Yeah – yeah, they're okay. I mean, they're a bit worried about him, to be honest. We have to take him to see a child psychologist.'

'How old is he?'

'Ten. It's a difficult age. He's had a few run-ins with other boys.'

'That's a shame.'

'There's one boy called Donnie and I don't know what it is but he can't seem to stop picking on him.'

'Oh right?'

'I think some boys just emit a signal. A softness. Bully me signals, you know?'

'Well, if you need any more time off come and speak to me.'

'Thanks Malcolm.'

Later, as everyone else is leaving the office and he is deep in his spreadsheet, he sees a meeting invitation from Malcolm pop up on his Outlook.

*

He watches. Every now and then he gets out of his car and wanders briskly round the block and back, slowing as he passes their house, peering into the windows. The curtains have been drawn but there is a thick chink between them. Through it he can see a small section of their front room, dimly lit, the television occasionally casting a coloured glow which lights up a dishevelled throw across a sofa, food packaging strewn across a coffee table. Occupying the far wall are, he can make out, a triptych of three large photographs, black and white but too dark for him to see.

He gets back into the car. On the radio a teenager who climbed Everest alone is being interviewed. He listens to the interview for a few minutes, then he turns the radio off and gets out of the car. He steps into the front yard of Yvo and her mother's house. If anyone asks him what he thinks he's doing, he will tell them that this is the house he grew up in as a boy, that he is reliving some memories which are very meaningful to him.

He moves towards the front door, watching the corner of the living room come into view. He can see the back of Yvo's mother's head, silhouetted by the television screen. They are watching a documentary about childbirth. He watches her for a few minutes. She stretches, runs a hand through her hair, leans forwards to pick something up, settles back.

He turns away from them, steps onto the front step. He turns around and looks out at Keith Street in the darkness.

*

'Sorry,' he whispers.

'What time is it?' she is groggy.

'Shhh.'

'God, it's nearly two AM.' She lifts her head from the pillow then lets it drop back down.

'I went for a drink. Malcolm insisted.'

'Are you drunk?'

'No.' He reaches beneath the sheets, rubs his hand up her thigh.

'No. Don't do that.'

'Why not?'

'Please don't.' She is half asleep.

'I can't help it,' he tells her. 'I'm drunk.'

*

He turns up the radio. 'I Want to Break Free' by Queen is

playing. He washes a mouthful of his egg and cress sandwich down with his Coke and sings along. But he doesn't know the lyrics so he just sings, 'Bom bom bom bom bom' along to the music.

He watches the television lights flickering dimly against the window. He has already wandered around the front of the house, but the curtains are drawn tight, no revealing chink tonight.

But there is light, muted light playing against the curtains. He watches that, chews, thinks. He thinks about the men he is researching. They too, he thinks, must experience lights such as these: suggestive of a secret depth, of an inner movement, baffling, fleeting. Could he contact them, seek it out of them? Find out what hides lit within them, note down what he learns, factor it into his data? Sales could use it. It could make the company a fortune, could put it on the map.

A movement to his side, just outside the house, a thud. He turns and freezes, feeling his heart pulse. Yvo's mother has come outside and pulled the door shut. She has come to speak to him, to ask him what he's doing, to tell him she knows he's been following her, after revenge for what her daughter did to her son. His fingers reach for the keys.

But no. She stops in the doorway, on the step. She lights a cigarette, folds her arms against the cold and looks out at the night. He watches the point of heat moving in the dark, from her mouth to her side. If she sees him, her body language doesn't give her away. She blows the smoke up into the air above her and watches it drift into the sky.

The Queen song comes to an end and is followed by 'Sacrifice' by Elton John. Quietly, he sings along, moving his head and his mouth as little as possible, watching Yvo's mother. And, when he doesn't know the lyrics, he sings, 'Bom bom bom bom'.

*

The sun is in his eyes. Malcolm says, 'So. No biggie. Nothing to worry about, but I've been speaking to Jez in Sales. He says he's still waiting for this month's report.'

'Yeah, it's actually not... I'm still working on it actually.'

'Still working on it? It was supposed to be with Jez,' he leafs through some print-outs, 'last Monday. That's over a week ago.'

'I know. But it's just not quite ready yet. It will be soon though. This week. I promise.'

'Well, do you have the names and phone numbers and job titles and all that stuff?'

'Yeah, it's all there. But I've been researching them. The guys on the lists. I've managed to find things about them. I thought if I could give Jez and all the sales guys as much information as I could find they'd be much more likely to make a sale.'

'Found stuff out? How do you mean?'

'Sort of personal stuff,' he says. 'How old they are. What they do outside of work. Whether they've been married.'

'Seriously?'

'I thought if Jez and all that lot had more information they could use it. They'd know what buttons to press, what to say. They'd make a sale.'

'I... I'm not sure I...' Malcolm sighs. 'What are you talking about?'

'So, there's this one guy. He's a director at an engineering company. But he's also into model boats. He builds them, spends months putting them together, takes them to boat fairs, wins awards. He's married. Has a daughter who's at university. She's studying Spanish. So, I thought Jez could use all that, you know? Figure out the guy's psychology, you know? All it takes is for-'

'Listen, could you just do me a favour? Could you just send over the list? Just the names with the phone numbers, job titles and the basic financial stuff? That's all we really need.'

'Yeah, of course.'

'I'm sorry.'

'Yeah. No. I just thought it'd be useful.'

'Yeah, and it's appreciated, but we need to get some sales notched up.'

'Yeah. No. Of course.'

'I know you've been having your problems at home. If there's anything you need, anything I can do to help, you'll let me know, won't you?'

'You what?' He says and laughs, shakes his head. He lifts a hand to his face because the sun is in his eyes.

*

He's woken by his seatbelt. It had been digging into his neck as he tried to shift around in his sleep. He undoes it, gets out of the car and stretches. The night is silent. He feels his phone buzz in his pocket. He takes it out and sees he has had missed calls, six of them, all from Carol. There are three text messages, two of which, he sees, feature Zak's name. He lets the screen go black. He wanders to the corner of the pavement, crouches and drops his phone through the grid.

He walks back to the house, steps into the front yard, stands on the step, looks out at the street.

After a few minutes he walks back to his car, then he stops and turns around. He walks back to the door. He stands looking at it for a moment, a hand out in front of him. He touches the handle, waits, lets go of it, touches it again, tries it, pushing down on it lightly. There's a click, quiet but decisive, as it gives, opening onto a murky hallway. It's messy, he sees. There are shoes haphazardly littering the floor amid scattered takeaway menus and unopened post. The door's progress is halted by a charity collection bag stuffed with clothes.

He steps inside and pushes the door to. He is careful where he treads but, as he rounds into the living room, he cannot help but step onto the corner of a DVD case left in the doorway, which lets out a single loud crack and causes him to slip slightly. He rights himself and stands still for a few seconds, listening for a response, a sound which lets him know he's been detected.

In front of him, he sees the three photographs. The room is dark but he can see quite clearly that they are each of Yvo – blurry, her face obscured by a strip of gauze caught in a strong breeze, her hair streaming out to one side.

In the centre of the room there is a coffee table. He crosses and sits in the armchair by the window, the one in which he had seen Yvo's mother sitting. He sits in it. There is, on the coffee table, a pewter tankard which is engraved with some writing. He pulls himself forward in the chair and leans forward to examine it. He treads on something and suddenly the room is brightly aglow. He has stepped onto the television's remote control. Thankfully, only a blank blue screen comes on. He lifts the remote and hits the power switch, but there is no response, the blue screen remains.

There is a creak somewhere above him, a carpeted thump, and then another. He stands up, tries the remote control again but it's no good. He crouches by the screen, hunting for a power button. There is another thump above him, the quiet rustle of movement. He locates the button and presses it, but instead of the screen going blank an image appears. A close-up of a man being interviewed on a beach. His voice blares out, so loud it causes the television frame to buzz. The man is describing how he has fallen out with his girlfriend: a reality show. Noisy music intersects with the images.

He hits the button again, and then again quickly, over and over: an advert for toothpaste, a film from the 1970's, the news, a music video. And in between each blast of noise, the sounds of someone approaching, crossing rooms above him and coming down the stairs.

'Who is it? Who's there?' calls the voice are on the staircase, Yvo's mother, straining to be heard over the music video. There is anger in her voice. There is a clunk of something metallic. A pipe being picked up? A gun being cocked? 'Yvo, stay there. Stay where you are.'

He hears her take more steps, coming closer. She is directly behind the door, stepping off the final step, about to enter.

'Stay there, Yvo.'

He drops back down into the armchair and watches as movement obscures the dull light at the cracks of the doorway. He picks up the tankard and leans back in the chair, nursing it – he moves his fingers across the engraved letters, trying to decipher them. He closes his eyes, settles back his head. The colours from the television play on his eyelids, and amid the sound of the music video – its loud synth, its low beat, its sampled saxophone – he can hear Yvo's mother. Her hand is sliding against the wood of the door as she eases it open and steps into the room.

Allowance

Dan Rhodes

I HAD ALWAYS GIVEN MY WIFE A GENEROUS MONTHLY allowance for contraception, so I was surprised when she told me she was entering the second trimester of pregnancy. Once the shock had subsided I found myself quite excited by the prospect of fatherhood. Even so, I couldn't help but wonder what she had done with all the money. She took my hand and led me to the cupboard under the stairs. Inside was a brand new vacuum cleaner. 'It'll help get things nice and clean for when the baby comes,' she said. She carried on talking, but I couldn't really hear what she was saying over the roar of the motor.

Bird-Tables for Swans

Lander Hawes

MAKING THE FIRST BIRD-TABLE ONLY USED A FRACTION of the wood. The design was the basic kind, found upright everywhere on the smoothed green of lawns. As anticipated, the table attracted the common garden birds, but in its position by the lake it appeared tiny and misplaced, tilting on the slope as if deposited by a receding flood. Still, I thought, gazing at the flitting blue tits through binoculars from the living room, at least I'd found a way to start using the rest of the planks and boards.

Even before the divorce, the quantity of wood had been a problem. Then, after promising to build the girls a tree-house, I'd let the warm summer weekends pass by, and Jenny had grown more and more irritated. Assuming I'd need at least two attempts, I'd half-filled a hired van with planks and boards, having to empty an outbuilding to store them. This particular outbuilding, the only dry and secure not occupied with my vintage cars, or shiny new gardening and DIY machinery, contained furniture from my dead mother-in-law's house, and Jenny was reluctant to see the armchairs and sofa she had such fond memories of moved to the cold grey cement of the barn floor, exposed to the damp chill of autumn and the busy incisors of rodents.

Eventually, I built the tree-house on the first attempt, finishing it the week before Christmas, but then Jenny left on Christmas Eve taking the girls with her, before I could reveal my special present. So the tree-house was left where it is now, alongside my deceased mother-in-law's dampening furniture, on the earth-cold floor of the barn. In fact, I completed the bird table by the end of December, and after telling my business partner that I needed some family time, I settled down amongst the snows of January into the ample space of the house and land, and all the equipment I formerly hadn't had the spare time to use.

I was interested if any of the larger freshwater birds might feed at the bird-table. The lakeside acres around the house backed onto a Wildlife Trust reserve, and migrating Canada geese and swans were forever flying and calling overhead, or landing on the water in great flapping, sliding splashes. It was clear, however, that a larger and sturdier model was required, perhaps a ramp and low platform so these birds could waddle up to peck and gobble. Whilst loading more wood into the trailer of the quad bike, I thought that once the interior was cleared I'd buy another vintage car and store it there, to console myself now that the family had abandoned me.

I next saw Jenny when she visited early in the New Year. She waited in her Range Rover, parked by mine on the gravel drive, until I descended the steps.

'Don't you answer your phone?'

'Sorry?'

I walked over, wiping my palms together, and smiling.

'I mean, why aren't you at work?'

'I told them I needed some family time.'

'What, now that we've left?'

Jenny looked at me as if I was a traffic warden ticketing her for waiting outside a school with the engine running. I thought she needed to apply some foundation and eye make-up, considering her age and the freezing weather.

'Do you want come in?'

'I need to fetch the girls' swimming gear.'

'Ok.'

She climbed out and stood, hands firm in the pockets of her quilted Barbour coat.

'Why are you covered in sawdust?'

After she'd gone I ate soup and bread for lunch and later returned to the workshop to finish cutting the bird-table frame. It resembled the base of a hen-house: a ramp elevating to a wooden square with a shallow trough in its centre. As I worked I imagined the birds clustering and squabbling, and also the slender, graceful necks of the swans when they settled to rest on the wood. I thought about hiring a digger to level an area by the lake, and how much the girls would like visiting and watching the birds feeding from the new table, all three of us together in the living room.

The next time I saw Jenny it was at the office of a marriage guidance counsellor that her solicitor had recommended. This counsellor was very interested in the events of last summer.

'So Mrs. Sutton, tell me again about the tree-house?'

Jenny hadn't been crying. Although tired, almost depleted, she sat very upright, and spoke in a measured way, as if describing symptoms to a doctor.

'Considering we'd hardly seen Evan for months, because of his meeting clients in the Middle East and Asia, I was hoping that he would see the tree-house as a way of reconnecting with the girls, and me too.'

'Do you recognise these feelings, Mr. Sutton?'

We both stared at each other.

'I'm sorry I don't.'

The counsellor made some notes on her papers.

'Well that's a very honest reply.'

'I came home all the weekends I could manage.'

Jenny shifted in her seat and swallowed.

'It was the summer holidays. The girls weren't at school.'

I began examining the nicks and cuts on my hands.

'Everyone in our family is very comfortable, Jenny.'

The result was that we agreed a schedule of visits for Josie and Elsa, and so the next weekend they spent Sunday with me. By then I'd finished the bird-table and positioned it by the lake. The girls came down and helped me scatter apples and mixed birdseed.

'Daddy, why is the bird-table so big?'

'The geese and swans are big too, sweety.'

'It looks like a landing place for a helicopter.'

The two girls shared a glance.

'Why don't we just put the apples in plant pots?'

After lunch we sat in the living room, once I'd moved the camp bed to the side, the one I'd slept on for the last couple of weeks. The girls played games on their i-Pad Minis, and I cleared up in the kitchen and served them coke with ice and lemon in tall glasses with straws. I heard Josie whisper to Elsa,

'He probably got someone to make it for him.'

They giggled, and didn't think to turn round to check I wasn't listening.

There was heavy snowfall on Monday and Tuesday, and the house became difficult to access. To pass the time I designed a bird-table for raptors and foxes. It was a sturdy post with an attached slit box and crossbeam with hooks, the box at knee level for the carnivores, and the beam higher for the birds of prey. For feed I shot three pigeons, hanging two carcasses from the hooks, and stuffed the other feathered bundle into the lower slit. To soften the frigid ground I lit a brazier on a spot near the other bird-tables, and later dug a narrow hole in the warmed earth with a trench spade, using a double-handed driver to hammer the post in.

Then, I spent most of the Wednesday sitting on the camp bed in the cold house, drinking soup from a mug and distracting myself by watching the swans and geese trundle up, or beat their wings in territorial displays. In the afternoon a buzzard perched on the crossbeam and fretted, shuffling to and fro for a while, before tugging one of the pigeons to its claws with its beak. In the twilight a fox bit at the remains in the box slit, tearing off a few bloodied morsels, and then an owl swooped into the other pigeon, knocking it to the dirty snow and feasting there. Watching all this, I wondered what other hungry creatures I could attract.

The next meeting with the marriage guidance counsellor was in early February. A pale, heatless winter light lit her office, and I was thinking it cast her lips and nose into etched ridges, as if this was an effect she'd dieted for.

'What do you think, Mr. Sutton?'

'Sorry. I was miles away.'

The counsellor smiled in a way that I imagine she had practised.

'We were just talking about the spring, and about moving forward.'

'Oh.'

'Mrs. Sutton was suggesting that you could build

something for the girls. She was explaining you like building things.'

Jenny had lost weight since the last meeting which made her look even older.

'Possibly.'

'What about another tree-house for your daughters? One for the garden of where they're living now.'

Jenny was clasping her hands in her lap and looking at me as if I was a kidnapper or a cellmate in a jail she was a newcomer to.

'I can try.'

'It would be so nice. You could put it in the old apple tree. Do you remember the apple tree?'

I glanced at the counsellor, and then back to Jenny.

'Kind of, maybe send some photos.'

She smiled at both of us as I tried to smile at Jenny.

'This sounds a little bit like a plan.'

I thought the counsellor might clap two or three times, the contact of her fingertips occurring parallel to her chin.

'Why don't you come next weekend, and take some measurements?'

I was sipping my tea and didn't acknowledge Jenny straight away.

'Yes. Of course. I'm not doing anything. In fact I might make a start before then.'

'Are you sure?'

'I think I know the tree you mean.'

So, on returning home I went into the frosty air of the outbuilding and considered what remained of the planks and boards beneath the raw blaze of the sodium floodlight. Fortunately there was enough for one more structure, and that evening I used my pencils to draft designs on sheets of A3 paper. The next morning I set about this final project; the cutting of the four sides was simple enough, but constructing the upper piece was much harder, and it was after dark before I laid the drill down and started lathering preservative on.

By lunchtime the following day this last bird-table was placed by the lake. It resembled a drawing of a lighthouse from antiquity in old-fashioned schoolbooks; a steep, four-sided pyramid collared by a wooden square fitted around the apex. For the feed, I spent the afternoon grinding two silver candlesticks from Jenny's mother's house into filings, and after driving into town to visit the butcher, my preparations were complete. Lying on the camp bed that night, drifting off, I thought of the pig's head atop the apex of the pyramid; the coldness of its skin, the moonlight gleaming off the silver filings I'd smeared on with glue. Then, in tipping into sleep, I imagined the circling approach of what was rare and airborne, the transfixed focus in the plunge of a descent, the thump and whoosh of air and wingspan, the screech.

Breakfast by the Motorway

Andrew McDonnell

H ERE WE ARE, ON A DATE.
Our last date together.

What venue have we agreed upon? A Gastro-pub? A loosely-ethnic restaurant someone vaguely famous tweeted about?

No, our last date together is at a Little Chef on the A14.

We've spiced things up though. We have a double date as we have brought along our respective lawyers. They are arguing over the bill and pushing the saucer with the free lollies from one side to the other. I'd pocket the lollies myself and give them to our kids, but they live with you now, and will just gather dust in the car ashtray.

Sometime soon we will leave this place and climb back into our respective vehicles. I will, no doubt, have an emotional moment when I look in the rear view mirror at the empty child seats. I'll take down the spy mirror so I can't see them, the tiny ghosts of what could have been: Holidays in Tiverton, sing-alongs on the M25, petty arguments over which films we will play on the portable DVD player.

Actually, I don't think I'll be emotional. I am past that stage now. But I can't help a bit of nostalgia, like our first date. I had sort of forgotten it, even though you hadn't. It was winter, possibly December; it felt like it belonged in the fag-end of a passed year. I had tried to trim my hair and ended up cutting it too short. I felt like someone else on that date, but, truth told, we try not to be ourselves on first dates, we try to be our PR agents. You might have worn a skirt. In fact it was a dress. It was florid. I think it was ugly; something an auntie might wear to a wedding. I remember a vivid memory of you either going to the bar or for a piss and I wondered how I would possibly touch you, how I would unpuzzle you. I don't mean that in a crude sense. I meant I was nervous - your sexuality and youthful vibrancy scared me. I was piloting a small plane that was caught in a downward spiral. I think I wore a black t-shirt; it was always what I felt the safest in, a £10 parachute from M&S.

Now I am lost in hostile land. I am not at the table, but amongst the £1.99 maps. I want to find this spot, this spot on the map where we will legally detach. Where I will only be woken by my daughters every other weekend; how this will be the pick up and drop off point; how they will bring their little carry cases of Peppa Pig figures and talk about people and places beyond my experience. I will suggest going out to Pizza Hut or the cinema. My child-filled weekends will be marked by excursions to out-of-town retail parks with their lurid colours and e-numbers, not the routines I became accustomed to, and that makes me feel heavy, as if something squats upon my chest.

Outside of the window, birds take berries from the central reservation. The road is pockmarked by frost damage, it reminds me of the muffin I pushed numbly round my plate. The scree from the road, the salt gritters and lorry spray has discoloured the windows, and etched into them unreadable runes. Something tells me that they tell it's not good.

Doug is your new man. You want to marry quickly; I know this as I was married to you. Doug is a dentist. Doug, I imagine, drives a Mercedes or some other status car. It probably has a vast bewilderment of things it can do. My daughters will drop their crumbs and plastic tops from their Ella's Kitchen into its valeted depths along with the odd toilet accident that will fail to blemish the leather upholstery.

But Doug will never see his dead parents in my children. He will never experience those strange moments, those unnerving times where someone you haven't seen for twenty years suddenly enters the room, or looks at you strangely when you tell them off. He will not get those moments, the ones that people never tell you about, that remind you of how alive you are, how the blood knocks at the wrist like a bailiff. Doug will not remember the forty-plus hours of labour or how one of the twins had to be resuscitated in the hallway right in front of him. Doug is childless. He has you, my little lights, on loan, not permanent transfer.

I have no Doug to go home to, no significant other. I don't want my own Doug. I just want to lie in my own bed and listen to the ringing in my ears.

I am pissing in the urinal. In front of me is an advert with some business people looking seriously at a PowerPoint presentation. They are all so sharp. I have never, despite my suits, felt that sharp. I have never been that focussed on a PowerPoint presentation. There is a blonde woman with oversized black frames and tightly slicked back hair. She is in a grey suit. One of the men, with suspiciously grey hair for one so youthful, is fist pumping the air with success. They make me feel sad, sad about the motorway, about modern life generally. Is this it? Is this all there is? Business people who don't exist in a restaurant where people come to divorce? I piss a little on the floor in protest but end up hitting the edge of the urinal and splashing my trouser leg and then having to use the hand drier to hide my shame.

Heading back to the table I can see all is done. 'We're done here,' says your lawyer. Congratulations I think. You are no longer Mrs. Wren. The twins will spend their alternate weekends playing I-spy on the English motorway system and trying to figure out what surname to use.

I am a Dad I told myself, over and over, the night I drove away from the hospital leaving you all there in the clinical light. I didn't feel like one though, you don't straight away. I tried in that small gap of time to savour the moments of my bachelorhood before you were all discharged. Sometimes I still don't feel like a Dad. I remember years ago a man on the radio saying he felt nothing, not an ounce of love or hate for his grown up children. He had done his bit and now he was getting on with his own life. The presenter called him brave. Then I read about another, a trawler man who on returning from the sea would weep uncontrollably and hold his family for so long that his wife had to hit him to bring him to his senses and send him to bed. He looked up his condition: Uxorious.

What kind of father would I be?

Thing is, we are shown model fathers all the time, playing with their kids and being strong, in adverts and films, everywhere. Would they ride on my shoulders or help me up the stairs when I become infirm? Who were these little people come to bury me? Truth is, I have always felt like I was acting through life, turning up to the rehearsal every day without fail, like a too-keen understudy waiting for his moment in the spotlight. As for being a father, I had no idea how to play the part.

Divorce seemed as inevitable as marriage. I could do nothing but conform. Once I realised I was losing you, I let go. Another man might have stood up and fought like mad for his family; said things that made the air electric, displayed an alpha-male ability to solve things with a few simple words.

Not me.

I had no lexicon for this. Even in hindsight there are no words I can find to fight back at moments already past, no great denouement to the final scenes of our marriage. No, the last meaningful words I spoke; the words that would determine the future of my family; the last few utterances that meant something were: 'How about the Little Chef on the A14?'

Somewhere, someplace, far on the edge of my vision, there is an audience wetting itself.

It's all done and my lawyer is shaking my hand in the car park. He's happy, and therefore I should be too. I feign happiness, but really I want to pull his glasses off, throw them into the motorway traffic and repeatedly punch him in the face. I've never hit anyone, but right now, I feel this urge to really hurt him.

But he is gone and I am left standing beside Ramage Haulage in the noise of winter traffic, a rising panic in my chest, a lolly in my hand; watching you pull away from me.

What Was Left

Samuel Wright

IN 1972, MY FATHER MARRIED FOR THE SECOND TIME. HIS first wife was in a coma, but he'd left her before that happened. They went for a picnic. Twenty-five people were there, with flowers in their hair and bottles of cheap white wine and little plastic bags filled with barbiturates. At four o'clock, some guests went to the riverbank, and dived in shrieking in their underwear. One of those who went swimming, a cousin or a friend's friend, dived in and never came out.

I don't know if this is true. My mother told me, but they separated in 1975. I was born three months later. I never met my father. Over the years, other things my mother told me about him included:

When he was born, he had webbed feet. Although the doctors said there was no point in operating, he disagreed, and cut the skin between with his mother's sewing scissors when he was six.

His first job was as a staff writer for a Marxist magazine edited by a pipe-smoking old Etonian who used to give him blow-jobs in the storage cupboard on press day.

When he and my mother argued, which they did frequently, the ultimate expression of his rage was to slap himself on the cheek, hard enough to leave five red fingermarks.

My mother was as strange as the stories she told. She wasn't lovable. She had skin that looked porous, and her eyes were liquid with emotion at home makeover programs, but hard and glassy when I cut my knee and came crying. She wore clothes that didn't look like clothes – trousers that had no clear division in the middle, jumpers that had more in common with rugs. When I read stories about boys who, on their eleventh birthday, were revealed to be guardians of the darkness, or chosen by fate, or otherwise more than where they came from, I longed to wake up and find that she wasn't my mother after all.

*

In my second year of university, I got stuck on the metro for three hours. I spoke to the girl in the seat next to me, and when we came up the escalator side by side, sweaty and blinking in the dusty sunlight, I asked her out.

On our third date, after I had kissed her once chastely and once with both hands at her cheeks like I was in a movie, she asked me to go home with her. I thought she meant her flat, above a kebab shop in Fenham, but she smiled and said, 'No, *home.*'

At two in the morning, by the open fire in her parents' house, I told her I loved her.

On our wedding day, we had an old-fashioned bus with a ribbon. Three people vomited, and one got punched. If anyone had sex, they did it in private. I had one moment of pure love, and another of total panic.

Waking up the next morning, I looked at Alice beside me. Her face was slack with sleep. Mascara had slicked down her cheek and traced fine black lines in the hairline cracks where her skin gathered towards her eyes. She looked deflated, soft. I kissed her on the cheek, and she smelled like linen and dust.

A few weeks later an undertaker called me up to say my father's ashes had been on a shelf in their storeroom for the last ten years, and would I please come and collect him.

*

The tin was urn shaped, but only vaguely. It was more like a hatbox. It had a screw top, and was surprisingly large and heavy. I took at home and put it on the table. I was sitting there, looking at it, when Alice came home.

'No one ever collected it?'

I shrugged.

'Did he have a funeral?'

I shrugged. 'I never met him.'

After that, it stayed in a cupboard for another seven years.

*

When I met childless friends and tried to describe what it was like to have a son, I said how, when he went to sleep on me, his hair sometimes grew sweaty, and it smelt like my hair, my sweat. I said how he felt, loose-limbed and stress-free, like a jointed toy. I said how he chuckled like the joy-switch had been flicked somewhere deep in his chest.

Other things I told people about him included:

The time he called cornflakes pornflakes.

The time he fell in love with digging, spent all day every day making muddy piles and finding scraps of stone and root, until he came to me holding a squashed worm and said 'Isn't this cute?'

The time he threw himself down the stairs, and my heart stopped, and we raced down after him, but after a moment's shock he giggled.

In the mornings, he came to our room. He'd call out and we'd fetch him, me one morning, Alice the next. I'd calibrate my waking up carefully so I could prompt Alice to get him instead without seeming to ask. I'd draw out my yawns, moving slowly so I could claim to be going if need be, and then settling back when she got up instead, hiding my excuses in mock sleep. The thing was, I never did sleep. Once she was gone, I'd just lie there, listening, wishing it was me he had wrapped his arms round.

On the days I did fetch him, I felt more awake than I could bear. The warmth of him set something off inside me. As I carried him I watched my feet, placed them with exaggerated care, felt my arms and the strength in my shoulders and held it, braced for disaster. The weight of him was a warning of the smack of concrete floors, the bend and twist of young bones breaking. His skin was too soft. Touching him felt like a dream of myself. On the sofa, in bed, I held his foot in my hand like I held my own. When he fell, and his skin split, the blood glittered like a nightmare.

When he was four, I watched him walk along a wall in the park. The spring air was still sharp, but the blossom had thickened the branches with dense white. It all felt green, new green, not thick, dusty summer green, old and knowing. We had walked the wall before, me holding him by the hand. I didn't that day. His feet stepped confidently, carefully. I watched him. He didn't totter any more, didn't lunge in that headlong lurching flight of the toddler, half way between a trot and a stagger. He balanced. When he lifted one foot to place it down, the rest of his body swayed with a smooth grace.

I stared at him. He looked like he could just step from the wall to the tree, and from the tree to the sky. He looked thinner and lighter than he'd ever been, almost invisible.

He looked up at me briefly, frowned and looked away.

All the rest of the day I wanted to ask him why he'd frowned. What he'd seen in me. But you can't do that with four year olds. At bedtime, I hesitated in the doorway until I heard his breathing ease into sleep.

After, I fetched the urn.

It was right at the back of the cupboard, hidden by rolls of old carpet and obsolete tents. It had gathered dust, thick and furry. I ran a finger across it, scraping up a line of dull metal in the fuzz. Then I wiped the whole thing, carefully. Dust still clung, so I took it to the sink. I cleaned it with a wet cloth, then wiped it in kitchen towel. I put it on the table.

'You should scatter them,' Alice said. She was standing by the door, watching me stare at the urn.

I took it to the Tyne. Upriver, to Hexham. There's a path by the river I like. It was late, so by the time I stood by the river no one was there. The air was damp and cold, the river big and quiet. When I unscrewed the lid I heard the scrape of grit in the thread. When I tipped it out it fell in a clump on to the surface of the water, sinking in dusty lumps and spreading a film of ash over the surface, looping in coils like oil. In the dusk I pictured a slim girl diving through it, the water folding over her without a trace.

I shook the urn carefully, then filled it with stones and sank it.

Back at home, I watched myself in the mirror. I checked the skin on the back of my hands. I eyeballed myself, looking for my mother, and then again, looking for what wasn't her. Sometimes, in the morning, I caught the smell from my armpits. My first illicit fuck took place three weeks later in the toilets of our local pub. It was momentary, a brief window of slick grunts, a turn of wet lips and the pulled tight string of a thong. Then back for more beer, a warm horror growing inside.

*

On the streets round our house, the blossom fell, the round petals scattered like someone dropped a hole-punch. The longer days brought squalls and sharp bright sun on damp tarmac. I began to walk to the metro in daylight.

Alice left me.

After a month, I met her in the park. My son wouldn't look at me, not at first. It took an ice cream, and a promise. We walked off together, ten minutes together. He stood by the wall, toeing the brick, staring at his ice-cream. The corners of his mouth were white. In his ear I could see the scatter of flecks of wax. When he was three he loved to clean his ears. When he was two he used to try to lick me, cackling and chuckling with his tongue out and his eyes sparkling with grubby merriment. I remembered his blood streaked from cuts, his snot, his shit under my fingernails.

I remembered that, but it was hard to remember how to speak to him.

'Your grandfather had webbed feet. Did you know that?'

He looked up.

'Like a frog.'

He looked up. He grinned, then the grin slipped.

'Do you have webbed feet?' he asked, seriously.

I was tempted to say yes.

'No.'

I thought of saying more. Inventing something amazing about myself. Even later, at home, I still pretended I might say it. I composed a letter – not a real letter, but an almost letter, unopenable. I said how we married in Hexham, his mother and I. No bus, no panic. Just the herons watching us hold hands in high summer. Gold sparkled on our fingers, in the long grass, in the river, clear, crystal water threaded with the silver bodies of fish and the sleek undying nakedness of swimmers. She wore white silk, and we danced in champagne to the buzz of autumn bees.

*

We never met, my father and I, but when I touch the ball of my thumb with my index finger, I feel the scatter and rub of him.

About the Authors

RODGE GLASS is the author of *No Fireworks* (Faber, 2005), *Hope for Newborns* (Faber, 2008), *Alasdair Gray: A Secretary's Biography* (Bloomsbury, 2008), *Dougie's War: A Soldier's Story* (with Dave Turbitt, Freight, 2010), *Bring Me the Head of Ryan Giggs* (Serpent's Tail, 2012) and most recently *LoveSexTravelMusik: Stories for the EasyJet Generation* (Freight, 2013). He is the winner of a Somerset Maugham Award and his fiction has been translated into Italian, Danish, Slovenian and Serbian. He's currently a Reader in Literary Fiction at Edge Hill University, also Programme Leader of the Creative Writing BA, and Fiction Editor at Freight Books.

LANDER HAWES' story 'Bird Tables for Swans' was shortlisted for the Bridport Prize 2014. His story 'Leaving France' was published in *Lighthouse Journal* in May 2015. An extract from his unpublished novella *What He Needs To Stop* was included in *Est: Collected Reports from East Anglia* in February 2015, published by Dunlin Press. In 2012 Unthank Books published both his story 'Differences in Lifts' in *Unthology 2*, and his novel *Captivity*.

RICHARD V. HIRST is a writer from Manchester. His work has appeared in the *Guardian*, *Time* Out and *The Big Issue*, amongst others.

TOBY LITT grew up in Ampthill, Bedfordshire. He is the author of four collections of stories, eight novels and, most recently, a book of essays, *Mutants*. His latest book of stories, *Life-Like*, also published by Seagull Press, was shortlisted for the Edge Hill Prize. *Life-Like* contains more stories about Paddy and Agatha, who first appeared in *Ghost Story*. Toby teaches creative writing at Birkbeck College. His website is at www.tobylitt.com.

ANDREW MCDONNELL was born in Shoreham, Kent and now lives in Norwich where he works in Adult Education. He writes poetry and short fiction. He is a director with Gatehouse Press and steers Lighthouse Literary Journal with a team of editors. He has two children.

COURTTIA NEWLAND is the author of seven works of fiction. His latest, *The Gospel According to Cane*, was published in 2013 and has been optioned by Cowboy Films as TV Serial for the BBC. He was nominated for the Impac Dublin Literary Award and The Frank O' Conner Award, as well as numerous others. His short stories have appeared in many anthologies and broadcast on Radio 4. He is associate lecturer in creative writing at Birkbeck, University of London and is completing a PhD in creative writing.

DAN POWELL is a full time father, part-time teacher and a prize-winning author of short fiction whose stories have appeared in the pages of *The Lonely Crowd, Carve, New Short Stories, Unthology,* and *The Best British Short Stories*. His debut collection of short fiction, *Looking Out Of Broken Windows* (Salt, 2014), was shortlisted for the Scott Prize and longlisted for both the Frank O'Connor International Short Story Award and the Edge Hill Prize. He is a First Story writer-in-residence and procrastinates at danpowellfiction.com and on Twitter as @danpowfiction.

R.J. PRICE's first short story collection *A Boy in Summer* was published in 2002, followed by a novel, *The Island,* in 2010. He is otherwise known as the poet Richard Price, whose collections explore family, love, and language, including *Small World,* 2012, which won the SMIT Scottish Poetry Book of the Year Award. He is Head of Contemporary British Collections at the British Library, London.

DAN RHODES has written six novels and three collections of stories, and won a bunch of prizes, including the E.M. Forster Award. His latest novel is *When the Professor Got Stuck in the Snow*. He saw The Smiths in concert in 1986. Now middle-aged, he lives just off the A6 with his wife and sons.

IAIN ROBINSON teaches in the School of Literature, Drama, and Creative Writing at the University of East Anglia. He writes fiction, essays, reviews, and literary criticism. His writing has appeared in *Litro Magazine, C21 Literature*, and *The Missing Slate*, and he has a story forthcoming in *The Lonely Crowd*. His novel *The Buyer* was published in 2014. He is also a prose editor for *Lighthouse Journal*. He lives in Norwich with his family.

NICHOLAS ROYLE is the author of *First Novel*, as well as six earlier novels including *The Director's Cut* and *Antwerp*, and a short story collection, *Mortality*. In addition he has published more than a hundred short stories. He has edited nineteen anthologies and is series editor of *Best British Short Stories* (Salt). A senior lecturer in creative writing at MMU, he also runs Nightjar Press, which publishes new short stories as signed, limited-edition chapbooks, and is an editor at Salt Publishing.

NIKESH SHUKLA's debut novel, *Coconut Unlimited,* was published by Quartet Books and shortlisted for the Costa First Novel Award 2010 and longlisted for the Desmond Elliott Prize 2011. His second novel, *Meatspace,* was published by The Friday Project. His short stories have featured in *Best British Short Stories 2013, Five Dials, The Moth Magazine, Pen Pusher, The Sunday Times*, Book Slam, BBC Radio 4, *First City Magazine* and *Teller Magazine*. He has written for the *Guardian, Esquire, Buzzfeed, Vice* and BBC 2. He has, in the past, been writer in residence for BBC Asian Network and Royal Festival Hall.

RICHARD W. STRACHAN lives in Edinburgh, and is a regular reviewer for the *Herald*, the *Scottish Review of Books* and *The List*. He has had stories published in magazines including *Interzone*, *Gutter*, *Litro* and *New Writing Scotland*, and by Galley Beggar Press. He was shortlisted for the 2015 Manchester Fiction prize, and in 2012 he won a New Writer's Award from the Scottish Book Trust.

TIM SYKES started writing a couple of years ago. This ended a decade and a half of prevarication, during which he had spent time living in St Petersburg and doing a PhD in Russian literature. He is currently working on a series of stories that draw on those wanderings in 1990s Russia. He now lives in Norwich and is dad to twin boys. They share their house with a cat but have not yet fitted a cat-flap.

SAMUEL WRIGHT is a writer and teacher. He has won the Tom-Gallon Award from the Society of Authors, been long listed for the Sunday Times EFG Award and the Manchester Fiction Prize, and had his stories published by Galley Beggar Press and Tartaruga. At the moment he is Head of a new Sixth Form in Sunderland.

Acknowledgements

The editor would like to thank the following for their advice and support: Richard Thomas, David Rose, John Lavin, Paul McVeigh, Joe Melia, Victoria Briggs, Tania Hershman, Ashley Stokes, Sean Preston, Matt Haig and Eddie Argos.

This book was made possible by the support of our backers on Kickstarter, who believed in *Being Dad* when it was still only a dream. Thank you to:

Dr. Roger Banks
Shaun Buhre
Sara Thompson &
   Alasdair Jones
Lindy Coxon
Eleanor Heck
Safia Moore
Colin Gray & Sara
   Bitenc
Sue & Chris Kopp
Francoise Harvey
Mike Showalter
Barry & Rebecca Ray
Cathy Holder
Glen Hammond
Steve Guise
Ruby Speechley
Catherine Watts
Catherine Yoshimoto
Ken & Wendy Sykes
Rupert Dastur
Steven Dick & Elliott
   Dick
Tom Oxley

Graham Russell
Michael Best
Dermot Walker
Leonard Sawyer &
   Christine Taylor
Suzette Thomas
Louise Prinjha
Jacqueline Smith
Alexandre Gil
Helen Rye
Fernando Bravo García
   & Mavilde Rebelo
   dos Santos
Marc Wright
Sam Mills
Mike Scott Thomson
Richard Sheehan
Open Pen Magazine
Martin Glass
Heather Findlay
Lewis Heathcote
Carlos Ezcurra
Layla Hirschfelt
Marc Jones

Maia Jenkins
S.A. Janis
Harold Rubin
Dominic Stevenson
Janet Olearski
Eric Holmes
Philip John Langeskov
Tamsin Cottis
Althea Joseph
Jane Roberts
James Cogan
Michelle Coxon
Bernie Deehan
Hilarie Johnston
Michael Christie
Hugh Bryden
Sandy Strachan
Ian & Heather
   Johnson-Lee
Audrey Meade
Julia Weller
Hugh & Christina
   Nicholson-Walker